Lola Lafon is a writer and musician. Born in France, Lafon grew up in Sofia and Bucharest, and now lives in Paris. *The Little Communist Who Never Smiled* is Lafon's fourth novel; it has been translated into eleven languages and won ten literary prizes in France, including the Prix Ouest-France Etonnants Voyageurs, the Prix Jules Rimet and the Prix Version Femina.

THE LITTLE COMMUNIST WHO NEVER SMILED

LOLA LAFON

Translated from the French by Nick Caistor

INSTITUT
FRANÇAIS
ROYAUME-UNI

This book is supported by the Institut français (Royaume-Uni)
as part of the Burgess programme

First published in Great Britain in 2016 by Serpent's Tail,
an imprint of Profile Books Ltd
3 Holford Yard
Bevin Way
London
WC1X 9HD
www.serpentstail.com

First published in France as *La Petite Communiste qui ne souriait jamais*
in 2014 by Actes Sud

Copyright © Actes Sud 2014
Translation copyright © Nick Caistor 2016

1 3 5 7 9 10 8 6 4 2

Designed and typeset by sue@lambledesign.demon.co.uk
Printed and bound by CPI Group (UK) Ltd, Croydon CR0 4YY

The moral right of the author has been asserted.

The Little Communist Who Never Smiled is a work of fiction. Apart from the
well-known actual people, events, and locales that figure in the historical narrative,
all names, characters, places, and incidents are the products of the author's
imagination or are used fictitiously. The novel does not purport in any way to be a
realistic interpretation of the historical events described.

A CIP record for this book can be obtained from the British Library

ISBN 978 1 78125 514 8
eISBN 978 1 78283 190 7

Mixed Sources
Product group from well-managed
forests and other controlled sources
www.fsc.org Cert no. TT-COC-002227
© 1996 Forest Stewardship Council
FSC

The little girls have laid down their rifles. They wade into the sea and dive in, sweat trickling down their necks, under their arms, along their backs.

MONIQUE WITTIG, *Les Guérillères*

I learned it then and have never forgotten this advice: Never tell the same story the same way to more than two people. Otherwise, when they reported back to the Securitate, you were done for.

ANONYMOUS, Romania, 1980

Foreword

The Little Communist Who Never Smiled does not claim to be a historical reconstruction of Nadia Comăneci's life. Although I have respected dates, places, and public events, beyond this I have chosen to fill in the silences of history and those of the heroine with traces of the many hypotheses and bootleg versions of that vanished world. The dialogue between the narrator of the novel and the gymnast is a dream, a fiction, a way of restoring sound to the almost silent film that constituted Nadia C.'s journey between 1969 and 1990.

L.L.

Part one

How old is she? the chair of judges asks the coach, unable to believe her eyes. The reply – fourteen – sends a shiver up her spine. What that young girl has achieved blasts away any progression of numbers, words and images. It defies understanding. There's no way of classifying what has just happened. She tosses gravity over her shoulder, her tiny frame carving itself a space in the air.

Why did no one tell them that was where they were meant to look, protest the spectators, who miss the moment when, on the ten-centimetres width of beam, Nadia C. throws herself backwards and, arms outstretched, launches into a triple back flip. They turn to one another: has anyone understood? Did you understand?

The electronic scoreboard shows COMĂNECI NADIA, ROMANIA, followed by a 73, her competitor's number, but where her score should be: nothing.

They wait. Pale-faced, the Russian gymnasts come and go in the rest area reserved for coaches and competitors after they have performed. They know. For their part, the little Romanian girl's team-mates look on as if in despair. Dorina has her hands clasped in front of her, Mariana mutters the same few words over and over, another girl has collapsed, eyes tight shut. As for Nadia herself, standing slightly apart from the others, ponytail askew, she doesn't even glance at the scoreboard. He is the one she sees first: Béla, her coach, arms raised skywards, head thrown back. She finally turns and sees the judgement: this terrible 1 out of 10 written in bright lights for cameras the world over to see. One point nought nought. In her mind, she goes over possible mistakes – perhaps the dismount after the somersault wasn't steady enough, but what can she have done to deserve this? Béla hugs her – Don't worry my love, we'll lodge a protest. Then one of the judges catches his eye. Look: the Swede is standing up. Look: he has tears in his eyes as he stares at her. And everyone will recount this moment over and over, so often that now she is no longer sure whether she actually lived it: perhaps she saw it on TV, perhaps the episode was written for a film.

The audience has risen to their feet, and eighteen thousand bodies unleash the storm. They stamp rhythmically on the floor, and in the midst of the din the Swedish judge's mouth opens and closes. He is pronouncing inaudible words, thousands of flashbulbs generate a shower of intermittent lights, she catches sight of the Swede: what's he doing? He's holding up both hands; the whole world films the judge's hands reaching out to her. So the girl stretches towards him, begging his confirmation… is it a 10? And here he comes, nodding gently, face hidden behind his raised fingers. Hundreds of cameras hide the child from him; the other young girls in the Romanian team are dancing round her – yes, my love, yes, that one point nought nought is a 10.

The scoreboard gyrates slowly from left to right, from the judges towards the audience, passing by the gymnasts, showing the number 1 that should read 10. A decimal point in the wrong place. Or rather, a decimal point that stubbornly refuses to be moved. A man is coming and going between journalists and judges. His official MONTREAL 1976 OLYMPIC GAMES T-shirt has dark patches under the armpits; he wipes his brow. The president of judges motions to him to come over, there's too much noise, something made the machine malfunction, I tell you; the whistling forces them to lean close to one another – are you joking or what? The whole world is filming, it's the first day of the competition. Where is that damned Longines guy? The engineer who designed the scoreboards clambers over the journalists kneeling round the little girl to reach the judges' table. They're gesticulating: your system doesn't work! And the Longines guy tells the IOC representative, who has cupped his ear to hear him – it works in the other competitions, *it works*, the computer doesn't make mistakes, you've caused the malfunction. He points a finger at the judges but everything has shifted, they're no longer paying him any attention. The judges have become spectators, they weep and applaud the girl sitting next to her coach, her narrow back turned towards the senile machine that is still grumbling: one point nought nought.

They go into a huddle at the break. OK. Did the Romanian or somebody on her team have access to the computers? Could she have swallowed something that possibly sent the system haywire? You're off your head, man, making things like that up just to cover yourself. Quite frankly, it's almost unbelievable! They blame each other. During the preparatory meetings the Olympic committee told us 10 didn't exist in gymnastics, protest the Longines engineers, whom the press have dubbed 'team one point nought nought'. At 13.40, the verdict: the computer database failed owing to the input of unusually high scores. The young girl has defeated the computer.

They have until the next day to adapt the computer system to the child. They push buttons, compile programs. An extra number has to be added. The decimal point moved to the right. What likelihood is there that she could do the same again, do you think 'that' could happen again tomorrow? I don't know, says the English judge. I don't know, says the Czech judge. They try to imagine exercises that would be worth 10 on the beam. Find it impossible. No one has ever scored 10 in Olympic gymnastics. They are asked a second time. Are you sure you weren't carried away by the spectators' enthusiasm? No, they reply. They really scrutinized the girl, trying to find any slip-up; there was nothing. No mistakes. More than that: some of the judges would have liked to go farther, to give her 11 out of 10! Twelve, says the Canadian judge. New numbers need to be invented. Or just abandon numbers altogether.

'If Comăneci were competing against an abstract standard instead of human rivals, could she still be given a perfect ten?' someone asks Cathy Rigby, a former gymnast who now works as a commentator for ABC. 'If Nadia were doing what she's been doing, all alone in an empty room, I'd still have to say that she would get the perfect ten,' replies Rigby, after thinking hard about the possibility of inventing an abstract standard more abstract than perfection.

They attempt to downplay what has happened. The following morning, the Olympic committee demands that Nadia take three additional drug tests. A debate rages: are we witnessing the emergence of a new generation of baby gymnasts, or is she one of a kind? It's a geopolitical earthquake. The Soviet coaches are taken to task: you mustn't let Romania humiliate us, Comrades. Ludmilla will save us! But that afternoon, Ludmilla finishes her floor exercise with a tragic, statuesque pose, a performance greeted with polite applause. Ludmilla rushes to sob into the arms of her coach under the Romanian's impassive gaze.

The elements are invoked: is she swimming in an ocean of air and silence? The sport itself is called into question: it's too brutal, almost vulgar compared to what is happening. They start from scratch: she doesn't sculpt space, she is space, she doesn't convey emotion, she is emotion. She appears – an angel! – just look at the halo all round her head, the glitter of hysterical flashbulbs, she rises above and beyond all laws, rules and certainties, a sublime poetic machine that blows everything apart.

Her routine is discussed: yes, it's true, there was already a foretaste of it with Olga at the 1972 Munich games, but now, with Nadia, it's the whole banquet in one go! Grace, precision, the sweep of her gestures, the combination of risk and power, and yet all of this seemingly effortless! It's said she can repeat her perfect routine fifteen times in a row. And that bone structure of hers... bones like silken threads. Morphologically superior. More elastic.

They search, play with words like these, then change their minds, try to encapsulate her. The little communist fairy. The little communist fairy who never smiled. They cross out the word 'adorable' because it's been used too often over the past few days, and yet that's what it is: painfully adorable, unbearably precious. And, obliged to look at her from our position as adults, yes, we wish we could slip inside her arduous childhood, stand as close as possible to her, protected as she is by her immaculate leotard, on which there is no sign of perspiration. 'An Olympic Lolita weighing barely forty kilos, a fourteen-year-old schoolgirl with the body shape of a young boy, who submits to everything demanded of her,' they write. We would love to anoint ourselves in the shower of sparks she gives off like a magical, boisterous toy. Tear ourselves from our sluggish, hormone-encumbered organisms. The little girl claws at our desire, we want it, oh, the desire to touch her, to be near her, a spiralling desire that is ever more urgent, and it's already over, the exercises on the beam lasted ninety seconds. Her fame spreads like an epidemic. For the finals, the ticket touts run out of the sixteen-dollar tickets they are charging a hundred dollars for; everybody wants to watch her, see her launch into her routines, so light you fear she will never come back down to earth. And when she sprints into her somersaults her elbows give her even more speed, the absolute firmness of her flesh squeezed into the white costume, she is this shooting mechanism wonderfully freed from her sex into a marvellously frictionless and higher childhood.

Things no longer look the same. Nadia is where it all begins. The other gymnasts are mistakes, the ideal deformed. The weight of years separating her from those who are beginning to be called 'the others', those who, the moment this child returns to the arena, nervously pluck at the fabric covering their buttocks. To hide away the flesh, hide what suddenly seems too much, incongruous, ridiculous even. Their leotards now seem too low-cut, too tight perhaps to contain the flattened chests of young women, chests that, as they run towards the vault, quiver imperceptibly. All that – breasts, hips, as a specialist explains when the event is retransmitted – slows down the twists, weighs down the leaps, spoils the figure. Ludmilla is 'terribly womanly'. In a photograph in a daily newspaper, next to the Romanian nymphette she looks disproportionately large. As for Olga, frankly it's almost embarrassing. The camera lingers on her, livid after the coronation of her Romanian rival. No, she isn't *tired*, she is *worn out*: she is twenty, almost – and you can hear the laughter of the other journalists in the studio – almost an old woman, she has too many miles on the clock, doesn't she?

Others knit their brows, let's be fair about this. A lady, yes, that's more like it, this Ludmilla is a *grande dame*. And after all, once upon a time Olga was a fairy too; one day Nadia will be going through what she is going through now. At the same moment the image freezes on the Romanian with the tiny face, the way she is nervously chewing her thumb, and a journalist murmurs to himself: 'Such small thumbs…'

Replay

The sound on the video seems to have been added later. As if someone had amplified the creaking of the bars she pounds with millimetric precision. They have been lent an echo that makes them an anguished, repetitive punctuation for her body as it folds itself around them. The little girl's lips tighten with the effort; her shoulders scarcely tremble at the impact when, after letting go and rotating on herself in midair, she catches the other bar. She balances for a moment on her hands on the higher bar. A triangle, a moving rectangle that becomes an isosceles and then an i, a line of silence, breath held, the geometric exercise is coming to an end, Nadia signals her dismount, her back hunches, knees tucked up to her chin for a double somersault only boys can achieve; until then it was as if you had been watching a sylph evolve, but now she's borrowing from the men and giving them the hiding of their lives. A woman's voice, a cry of insane joy, escapes from the mass of eighteen thousand spectators. It punctuates the feet in their white gym shoes that land on the floor without the slightest waver. Her arched back is a comma, rising to the tips of her fingers when she tickles the sky, she salutes. And the computer scores 1.00 again, as she runs towards Béla, who is holding his arms out to her.

Now she is pirouetting on the beam, illuminated by the flashes of crazy fireflies, a dancing light. The child seems to hold everyone's breath. She finishes with a double twist punch and, with a snap of the fingers – her dismount is impeccably stable – she sets them free, as if the volume button has suddenly been turned up from mute, and the public roars with a delight mingled with relief that she hasn't fallen. Then they all rush for the press room, the telephones, *10, 10*, make sure you get that, *she's perfect*, reads the headline in *Newsweek*, it's never been seen before, perfection is of this world. 'If you're looking for a word to say that was so beautiful that it was impossible to describe how beautiful it was, say it was *nadiesque*,' writes one Quebec editorial writer. The judges are obliged to ask Béla exactly what exercises she performed, they were too quick for them to follow.

It is midnight in Oneşti, a town in Romanian Moldavia to the north-east of Bucharest. On the screen, the child runs, a small, aggressive machine driven on by all those encouraging her to obliterate the beautiful Soviet ballerina, whose movements in comparison seem soft, lascivious.

Stefania has hidden under the dining-room table, burying her face in her hands, shuttering her eyes as a precaution; Grandma and Gheorghe tell her to stop her nonsense. A furious wave of sound engulfs the television set, the saturated noise invades the room, and Stefania, cheeks bright scarlet, is desperately anxious: What is it, Gheorghe, tell me: did she fall, tell me, did she fall? Her husband kneels down gently beside her, takes her hand to help her stand up and murmurs: Look, look. In slow motion, their child's frail body slices through the air, dislocated, the lunacy of her leap dissected moment by moment. Stefania sobs and stretches out her hand towards the tiny silhouette which, back turned, salutes a crowd of thousands of weeping adults.

Mission accomplished

They are waiting for her. This first press conference is packed out, all five hundred seats and more on the ground, there is no room anywhere. The walls are covered in embroideries of flowers. When she finally arrives, dressed in the Romanian team's tracksuit with blue, yellow and red bands and the hammer and sickle on her chest, her coach lifts her and carries her at arms' length to her place; the doll she is clutching is wearing the same tracksuit and their hair is done up in the same way, with two bunches tied up with red ribbons. Above her head, a portrait of President Ceauşescu.

The journalists can ask Nadia any questions they like, announces a friendly young woman with a strong Romanian accent. At her feet – there are no more chairs – these adults adjust themselves to her level. Do you like chocolate, Nadia, a few words in French, please, in French! Bravo! Do you play Monopoly, Nadia, do you have a boyfriend, Nadia? It looks as if they might start sucking their thumbs at any moment, when they spot her cute pointed canine teeth (could they be milk teeth? No, she's fourteen). Again, Nadia, again, as she mimes the judge who, seeing her distraught at the one point nought nought, holds up his ten fingers. Ten! *Great*! And now she has achieved perfection, what does she want to do next? I can do better, she promises seriously, clutching her rag doll to her, under the watchful eye of her coach, a big, affable-looking fellow with a thick moustache. That no doubt means she'll have to invent another sport, they say to themselves. Are you surprised at scoring 10, Nadia? She shrugs her narrow, straight shoulders and chirrups in Romanian, 'I know it was perfect, I've already scored ten, it's nothing new.' Could it be she misunderstood? They ask her again. Are you astonished that you won everything? She shakes her head. Do you feel sorry for Olga and Ludmilla? She repeats firmly, No, not sorry. They try another tack. 'How did you celebrate your victory last night?' Almost annoyed, she purses her lips. 'I didn't celebrate anything. I was sure I would win at least one title. I went to bed.'

'Which is your favourite exercise?'

'The uneven bars, because I can do skills the others will never be able to do!'

And… Couldn't she smile a little? She sighs. I'm sorry, but if my foot touches the edge of the mat after a diagonal of saltos, even by only three centimetres (she raises a hand and holds up her thumb, first and middle fingers) I lose points. So yes, she can smile, but only when her mission is accomplished. Laughter breaks out in the room, followed by applause: it's so cute to call it a mission, Colonel Miss. An English journalist maintains she is merely emulating Olga K.'s technique, but he is immediately interrupted by the coach. 'We represent the Romanian school, we don't copy anyone.' Some of those in the room try to calculate how much of a child she is. Her expressionless face when she performs, her coolness: as soon as she saw her score, she put on her tracksuit, a mini-functionary of acrobatics! And the other morning I ran into her in the Olympic village, she was having her medical, her eyes didn't blink once, no expression. What does she have to tell us? She likes yogurt and doesn't eat bread. Great. She's a forty-kilo communist robot. Sure, she does have a certain grace, but it's a metallic, efficient grace, a long way from the lyricism of the Soviet girls, oh no, forget swans and Tchaikovsky, these

Romanian gymnasts are puppies being made to do tricks, they perform them and serve the State. It's a question of geometry, of computation.

They start to miss the older models. Olga, for example, who at the Munich Olympics simpered in a really exciting way and sniffled if she fell, then there was Ludmilla, who won everything, a calm Soviet lady. The classical dance tradition of the huge USSR undone by an obscure satellite country now crowned as the specialist in perfectly trained young girls (that tragic episode when the beautiful Ludmilla from another century tries to hide her tears from the reporters in the arms of her coach, while right in front of her the snotty little brat struts up and down, terrifyingly skinny).

The child has to rest before the final disciplines, they leave the press room laden with gifts, plum brandy, magnificent fabrics from Transylvania, the Romanians know how to do things. They meet colleagues who couldn't get in, tell them about this pale spectre, from her white leotard to her chalk-covered hands, not forgetting her face drained with fatigue. Everybody returns to their hotel rooms to finish the article they have to send that night, they didn't get very much out of the press conference. In the hotel salon, the TV quickly resumes the day's events to get to the real news: there is only one story, and that's her. A young woman hurriedly turns up the volume, Nadia begins her floor exercise.

And they realize that this is something else. This skipping charleston she is performing to, this 'Yes, Sir, That's My Baby', a tune full of a pre-1929 joy, *yes*, *yes*, *yes*, our little cheat is dealing a sly hand, shuffling the possible, *yes*, *sir*, look, she doesn't even use her hands for support from the ground when she leaps, the air itself holds her up, *my baby*, and everyone is convinced that yes, *that's my baby baby*, she manipulates and rearranges childhood to perfection, the little tramp from old Charlie Chaplin films, you want to take her head in your hands. It's so joyful. Light as the air. And that lifts some of the heaviness of the security surrounding these Games haunted by the massacre at Munich, the hostage-taking and the killing of Israeli athletes. The little girl has just taken us by the hand and together we are turning and turning in a spiral of insouciance. She salutes the crowd on her feet, the sulking Russians leave the hall in a line behind their coach, while Béla thrusts out his fists, punching the air in his delight, sur-rounded by little girls jumping all round him, their eyes circled by lack of sleep, their mouths parched with hunger. The child is carried off in triumph, they will even go down on their knees if necessary before this elf five foot nothing tall, who sweeps away the machine guns bristling all over the Olympic village. She has saved their bloated Games: 9,250 athletes, accompanied by 3,235 assistants spied on by more than 8,000 journalists, and 16,000 sol-diers meant to prevent an attack by the Baader-Meinhof group, Carlos, Japanese kamikaze, the IRA or Palestinians or even, pos-sibly, Quebec separatists.

So, empty with the calm after a celebration, already missing the Carpathian fairy, millions of mothers switch off TV sets that have been on constantly since the 17th of July. They start to dream of having a daughter like that, so slight, a pale child so anxious to get things right, good, serious, hard working, sober, never kicking up a fuss, someone who climbs onto podiums and makes huge medals shine on her flat, firm chest, who waits for her score in front of cameras from the world over, after enchant-ing millions upon millions of TV viewers, finishing her routine with that pose that has become a postcard on sale everywhere, a child who comes from an odd country, Romania, a child who has submitted herself to a life of discipline, for whom you buy bows to tie prettily around her hair, someone adorably smooth and odourless, this desire to have a little girl shut off from the world, unaware that you can do nothing for her and who soon, oh so very quickly, will be engulfed by her humdrum biological fate.

So, empty with the calm after a celebration, already missing the Carpathian fairy, millions of little girls switch off TV sets that have been on constantly since the 17th of July, as though stunned by a prolonged absence. In front of the mirror in the corridor, they improvise a triumphant salute, arms aloft, spine stretched so far that their chests puff out, T-shirts showing the skin squeezed by the elastic of their nylon knickers. In their dreams their bodies become as swift as hers. That evening, little girls in the West turn down a second helping of potatoes and refuse a dessert, filled with a secret mission, to spread the white, that marvellous white of the leotard, the chalk and the sacred life of Nadia in the snow, yes, there must be snow over there where there is nothing.

Following my request for other people's accounts when I embark on this undertaking, I receive dozens of letters and even more emails from fans of Nadia C. Most of these women are aged around forty, but others are very young and cannot have been old enough to see her live at Montreal. All of them, though, remember the shock. Their amazement when Nadia C. causes the computer to malfunction. Their sudden distaste for cereals with too much sugar in them, those packets filled with throwaway mini-gadgets, this kind of abundance out of place in their new realm of heroic deprivation. Their refusal to wear skirts that are so unsuited to playing at being Nadia C., whose white leotard becomes the accusatory mirror of their soft lives lacking in any sense of duty. Because Nadia C. is not only light. She is powerful, ruthless. Nadia C. never smiles, never says thank you, it is adults who beg her to concede them a glance. She says nothing, distant and focused, surrounded by adults in tracksuits, strange gym teachers who congratulate her respectfully. The girl who comes from a country that no one, not even parents, had heard of before it was mentioned on TV. Nadia C.'s poster belongs to the young girls of the summer of 1976. The boys pin Farrah Fawcett up in their bedrooms; below her amber-coloured costume, her tanned thighs are spread slightly open, warm and inviting.

In our first telephone conversation, I make it clear to Nadia C. that this account will not necessarily be faithful, that I am allowing myself the liberty of filling her silences. We agree I will send her the chapters as I complete them for her to give her opinion.

Dear Nadia,

In response to your questions: I go into the details of your relationship with Béla further on. The chronology? It seems to me I have to start with Montreal, I'd almost say to get it over with. As everybody knows of it, or at least has a memory of it. But we can talk about all that during the week; I'll give you a call. Here's the next part of the story, or rather, the beginning!

Yours...

A field of Véras

Three years of filling in forms to create this experimental gymnastics school where calculation will go hand in hand with learning the uneven bars. Three years of meetings with officials in Bucharest who have to be showered with gifts to make any progress, American bourbon a customs officer friend of Béla's confiscates from diplomats, ham from the countryside. And now that they have found a place in the small town of Oneşti, there are only thirty young girls who correspond to what Márta and Béla are looking for. The Gymnastics Federation is astonished, annoyed, there's no shortage of young girls who want to be part of the school, what's the point of this over-demanding selection process! And then it's always 'girls'. Why refuse to take this boy who can stand on his head and jump higher than his sister? This business intrigues people in high places. What is it, this girls-only sport, comrade?

Is it a theory? An intuition? An observation? It's an idea that takes shape the previous year, when Béla and Márta visit competitions in neighbouring countries, noting each gymnast's strong points, their weaknesses, the different music used, the routines the public like. In the Soviet Union, gymnastics is spoken about in the idiom of classical dance, whereas in Hungary or Bulgaria, the girls' gestures are broad and sporty; peasant girls from the mountains out for a healthy walk. If they began younger, they could take part in three Olympiads, exclaims Márta enthusiastically.

The most renowned Romanian gymnasts are in their twenties, and most of them lose interest in competing once they are married. 'All that investment, all that time spent training housewives whose only thought now is to spread their legs and do the cooking,' rages Béla as they are leaving their nth competition, 'and it's as boring as the fucking ballet, are they afraid of messing up their hairstyles or what? Even my grandma can do forward rolls better than them!' Furious at the competitors' soft prudence, he sits with Márta on a bench in the nearby park. 'I much prefer to watch these children play!'

These out-of-breath children hanging awkwardly from a tree branch, incapable of imagining they might fall, little ones you're constantly afraid might plunge to the ground. And who you can't help but watch, despite your fear. Or precisely because you are afraid, because they could break. And yes, the little boys know how to jump and run more quickly than the girls, they like to show off their abilities, whereas the girls often timidly try out the steps they have been taught. But a brave, leaping boy is still nothing more than a boy. Whereas a girl… Light and more supple, she needs only to be taught fearlessness.

'Have you seen Véra compete, comrade, Véra Čáslavská?' Béla asks the bureaucrat in charge of his file who is asking him about the wisdom of a school reserved only for girls. Of course! Everyone knows the great Czech champion, even if in the summer of 1969 one suspects that the new Czech regime will never allow her to go abroad again after the Olympic Games in Mexico the year before, when she deliberately turned her back on the Soviet flag right in front of all the international media, a scandal. And then the Hungarian – who, the bureaucrat remembers, appears to have access to an inexhaustible stock of foreign alcohol – starts roaring at the far end of the line: I'll give you whole fields of Véras in my school, all you'll have to do is pick them! Frankly, comrade, can you imagine boys, their whatsits squeezed into their leotards, in the middle of my beautiful fields of Véras? Enough about your studs already, please; when I come to Bucharest we can drink to the Véras!

The apparition

For this first school year, a crowd gathers outside the new building. The parents of the girls who have been selected, the sceptics too, all of them want to see him, this Béla who has just come to live in Onești with his wife. Béla. A Hungarian name, from Transylvania, no doubt. It's said he was once a champion hammer-thrower and a boxer, he also plays rugby, and was a member of the national handball team... But what about gymnastics, the parents fret. Oh, his wife knows about dance, anatomy and dietetics. For his part, Béla tried for two years to learn to keep his balance, but it only ended in a fall that put a stop to his schizophrenic illusion of lightness. But he is really likable, this moustachioed giant who lifts the little girls in his arms and claims he can breathe life back into Romanian gymnastics, which has been asleep for years now. He slaps the doubters on the back and spits on the ground whenever the Soviet champions are mentioned.

They have promised results to a low-level apparatchik short of whisky who with a single zealous memo can have the school closed. No time to lose. For twenty-one days, Béla and Márta put the young girls to the test. They think they are playing when races are organized between them to judge their speed. Some of them learn to walk on their hands after barely a week; in the second week they are told how to make a bridge with their back and do a back flip. They have their hand held when they climb onto the beam for the first time, they advance cautiously across its ten-centimetre width. At the end of the third week, Béla retains only five names. Of which one has a question mark against it. The others? They cried when they fell. They clung on to him and refused to let go. Others collapse giggling on the ground in the middle of sets of press-ups, grimace when he is gauging their suppleness by raising their leg in front of them little by little. It's not so much their reticence that leads him to rule them out. It's because they show it openly. He now knows more precisely what he is looking for, but still has not found it.

Until late one morning, in the yard of that primary school in Oneşti. Years later, Béla has refined his account of how they met. He always begins it with: he knew the moment he saw her. He could add that the moment he saw her, she escaped him, vanished. The dark-haired girl who one Thursday morning in the yard turns a very promising cartwheel against a low wall. She has bunches, he tells himself, trying to recall a detail that could identify her as the children run to line up in pairs – the bell has sounded. But they all have bunches, it is 10.15 and the sky-blue blouses slip away into the darkness of the classrooms, among them, that one.

He opens every door, class after class, apologizing for taking the teacher's time, risking a 'Who likes gym here?' Sometimes it's a boy who raises his hand. 'Who here can do a cartwheel?' he asks tirelessly, sensing that, on top of his fatigue, he is growing frustrated at not finding the girl again. Delighted at this break from routine, many of them want to demonstrate for the gentle-man, the ordinary mediocrity of their movements touches the teacher, but Béla can feel himself growing irritable and leaves the classroom as a plump little girl tries a second time to do a cart-wheel, no point lingering. It's the last class on the upper floor (or does he choose, seven years later when he is telling the story to the journalists, to say it was the last, to create an effect – do you see how it all depended on that instant?)

Yet again he asks, Who knows how to do a cartwheel, and from the back of the room several hands are raised towards him. The brown-haired girl's bunches are slightly askew, they must have come loose in a game. 'You two, can you show me?' They whisper something in each other's ear and, glancing at the teacher to make sure that they really do have permission to stand on their hands in class, they get up. To the right. To the left. The brown-haired girl doesn't even look at him, she is caught up in her exercise, which she does a second time, encouraged by the applause from the other children. Comăneci Nadia and Dumitriu Viorica. Their parents' permission given in September 1969. Day pupils.

That remark by Béla about gymnasts of those days 'who were afraid of spoiling their hairdos' is the opposite of what it seems, a misogynistic joke, Nadia assures me when we discuss this chapter over the phone.

'They really were worried about not being "feminine" enough, because grace and appearance were what the judges were looking for in the girl gymnasts. Perspiration was reserved for male gymnastics; the females were not supposed to look too athletic... Béla couldn't care less whether we looked pretty, each week he would choose the most reckless among us, and the quickest. We all wanted to win the medal... What he valued was our strength, our courage or our endurance, not our hairdos! I think that's why he wanted to work with such young girls, because we hadn't had the time to learn those... rules.'

1969

When they are admitted to the school, a doctor examines the two little girls; they have only kept on their white knickers, and the cool tiles under their bare feet make them fidget and hop on the spot, they have to be scolded. They are told to hold their arms out to the sides, their span is calculated. Then they are shown how to touch the ground with their hands. They are measured. Hips narrower than shoulders. It is explained how they are to spin round as quickly as possible and then walk towards a fixed point in the room to assess their sense of orientation in space. They are prodded. While they are grasping the wall bars, their legs are raised in front of them until they wrinkle their noses.

Very few girls can keep their eyes fixed on an invisible line, their faces taut when more pressure is put on. Some bend their knee to avoid the discomfort of a muscle stretched too far, or wriggle. What about her? She's got guts, he writes in his notebook, that's for sure, but there's nothing extraordinary about her. She doesn't complain when he sits – taking care not to put his whole weight on her, she is only seven – on her back while she does the splits, stomach pressed against the floor. She runs round the gym clenching her fists, stops as soon as she is called, enjoys responding to instructions, to salute, her chest arched like a parenthesis. For weeks she quizzes Márta, 'Madame, will we be on the big beam by Christmas?' because she's disappointed she has to learn to move on a line chalked on the floor, then on a very low beam surrounded by mattresses.

After three months, they are called in with their parents. Nadia's mother has put a handkerchief in her handbag for the little one, she hopes this ceremony (a formality? A judgement?) won't go on for ever, she has appointments with two clients to take their measurements. Winter is approaching, and orders are picking up, coats in the 'Paris' style that are in great demand among the women of Oneşti who take a folded page from a Yugoslav fashion magazine out of their pockets.

In the gym, to a soundtrack of recorded music, they are marching, chins raised, all of them in blue leotards, Nadia's is too big for her. Following the speech by the mayor, congratulating himself for having brought to the town this experimental school that will create the elite of socialist gymnasts, Márta calls out the names of fifteen young girls. She shakes hands with those who have not been accepted, and they run and throw themselves sobbing into their mothers' arms. The five chosen ones congratulate each other excitedly; through the window at the back of the room the sun draws a fleeting line on their chalky white thighs.

Late that evening, she finally falls asleep (they celebrated her being chosen; in the living room Nadia shows them how she can walk on her hands, until she knocks over a lamp) with her rolled-up leotard pressed against her cheek on the pillow.

1970

It would be wonderful to say everything progresses in a straight line, to follow with amazement the obvious trajectory of a magical little girl. But there is that 23 June 1970, her first participation in a national competition.

Nadia steps forward, a tiny, martial, eight-and-a-half-year-old figure, salutes the judges to show she is ready.

She is on the beam. Haggles with gravity over a handstand. Márta's final recommendations ('Show them all!') form ribbons inside her head that slow her gestures. She has dreamed of this so often. The room has fallen silent, the dry crunch of the soles of her feet, the puff of chalk against the wood each time she turns. And it is the little girls sitting on the bench, the ones who have already competed, who are the first to cry out, like an ancient tragic choir, and provoke the public's 'Oooh' at the moment when Nadia falls to the right of the beam.

Grim-faced, she uses both hands as she has done in training and climbs back on to the apparatus. Hardly has she attempted the hateful leap again than she falls off a second time, to the left this time. Béla rushes up – Come to Papa, sweetheart, come here, to help the littlest of the little girls in the school, the one who never tires, who continues the exercises long after his ritual 'That's enough for tonight'.

And that is what Béla will recount hundreds of times over the next twenty years: she attempts that salto again as if she has to strike out the image of her fall, her cheeks as red as if she has just suffered a string of horrible insults. And falls again. The tiny child raises herself a fourth time onto the beam that is too high for her. Smiles all round, they take pity on her strained face. Her hands beat the air, her body barely fills the sky-blue leotard. But the silence she re-establishes in this provincial gymnasium. Her determination to secure the few tenths of a point she will be awarded if she continues. Pride and her arrogant gaze, even more intense than at the start of the exercise. Now she sashays along the beam with secure, precise steps. The laughter has died away. She is there in person to blot out, wipe from their memories, something she herself does not appear to remember. And the only thing she leaves out, after her perfectly executed dismount, is her salute to the judges.

On the bench, Viorica and Dorina are crying, convinced Nadia's slip-ups will cost them first place in the team competition. Her brows knit, Nadia doesn't talk to anybody. When one of her team-mates reaches out to one of her ruffled bunches, Nadia stands up abruptly and moves away to await her score. It is a poor 6.20, but Béla raises his arms like a boxer at the end of a fight. Had Nadia only scored 6, their rivals from the town of Oradea would have won, but that 0.20 makes all the difference.

Sometimes, in a corner of the gym, Nadia, foot pointed forward, chest thrown out, throws herself into a perfect hand-stand; she has mastered how to perform on her hands from the age of seven. But you would have to get very close to her to see how her wrists tremble and to hear her counting, head down, abdomen taut, breath held, in order to hold her position a few seconds longer. During these early years, it is her organism she is painstakingly constructing, testing the efficiency of the articulation of her joints, of every detail before use. If she is scolded, she listens, an engineer eager to correct any faults in the installation, so serious she seems colourless.

When Nadia fell off the beam, Márta cried out. The humiliation of that ridiculous clowning in front of all those people, the little squirt has really come a cropper, her fear was palpable right up in the stands. Márta is so furious that her words run away with her. On the train home, she regrets her outburst, and leans over the sleeping Nadia, pushing back the hair from her eyes, it was so hot that summer. In her sleep, the child starts and turns away, curling up into a ball, as though brushed against by a wild animal.

Junior friendship cup

May 1972

All six little girls from Onești climb onto the podium in second place, silver medals round each of their necks. In the photo, the Czech, East German and Soviet gymnasts weigh on average twenty kilos more than the Romanians, these orchid-soldiers whose hair Béla has adorned with big red ribbons, the sweet little vertebrae plainly visible beneath their sky-blue leotards. Ludmilla Tourischeva, the Soviet champion, is eighteen. The Russian press talks of a 'polemic surrounding the age of the competitors'; under a photograph of Béla, the caption reads that 'the Romanian' had no idea the other competitors would be young adults.

A few days after their return to Romania, Béla and Márta call Nadia into their office over the gym. Béla is occasionally worried that she is ill, that silent pallor of hers, that fixed stare contrasting so strongly with the determination of the tiny body to unpick the difficulties of an exercise until she has completely digested them. She is an anaconda, voracious for risk. They can never feed her enough.

Márta and he have seen more than enough girls who lap up everything they're shown without so much as drawing breath, allowing their limbs to recite the difficulties. The same ones who, a few weeks later, expect their hair to be stroked, to be showered with compliments, or at the end of the training session have their future of national glory outlined for their parents. Márta knows that there's nothing to be gained from this sentimental rubbish. It would take too much attention, too much encouragement, too much coaxing to achieve what they are after, spending time on these 'sensitive' girls – the word she writes in pencil in her notebook next to a name underlined in red: sensitive, the definitive judgement. But Nadia doesn't even blink when they raise their voices. She is never heard. She is never noticed. It's as if she is absent in the unmoving hours.

Nadia is making progress. You didn't fall, two gold medals is good, sweetheart. And yet. This progress is fragile, you have to work harder than the others.

At night over supper, she pushes her plate away and asks her mother if she can go to bed. Stretched out on her back, her tears trickle down to the pillow, a silent punctuation of the words she whispers, 'Parachute jump, pa-ra-chu-te', before she falls asleep thinking of this image Béla has given her of how to approach the dismounts she is still wary of.

During my first year at the school, Márta told me one evening: Close your eyes, imagine your legs are paint brushes, and draw a single line, above all making sure you don't make any mistakes! The next morning I was very anxious, and told her, 'Madame, I fell in my dream last night.' And Márta congratulated me: Fall, sweetheart, and get it over with, we won't mention it again. Could you include that in your chapter, please?

October 1974

S he calls her parents from Varna, where the World Championships are being held. She can't take part because she is too
young. She complains about everything, the journey, the weather,
Béla, the gym. She is even missing her younger brother, although
she never pays him any attention when she's at home. She hangs
up, promising to go to bed so that she won't miss her train the
next morning.

In November she will be thirteen. Sometimes Gheorghe and
Stefania don't know how to speak to this child of theirs. How to
respond when she spits disdainfully that she is 'hors concours' as
if it were a shameful disease. They rarely go to see her train. Have
only seen one competition. They are unaware that a French journalist, that same morning in Varna, dazzled by the 'hors concours'
display by the Romanian team, has asked to meet Béla, but as no
interpreter is available, he cannot in the end invite the coach on
to his TV programme, which he begins with 'I have seen a young
Romanian who, if everything goes well, will no doubt become
one of the world's greatest gymnasts.'

'Did you know at the time that you were one of the best?'
'No… I heard rumours, there was talk that in the team there
was a girl who was really good. But I didn't know it was me.'

When I discover an archive article telling the story of the gymnastics *gala in Paris, I find it so hard to believe because everything in the account seems to me already to have been rewritten for the legend, scripted: the aberration committed by the French Gymnastics Federation, which invites part of the Romanian team to a prestigious gala, but which, when it discovers how young the gymnasts from Onești are from photocopies of their passports, sends them to a demonstration by junior beginners.*

Over the telephone, Nadia confirms every detail of this epic. I sense she is still amused by their adventure, and expects me to feel the same way. A few days after our conversation, when I find I am unable to write about the episode with the humour she would like to find in it, I get back in touch with her and confess I am concerned by Béla Károlyi's instruction to Nadia to perform extremely dangerous skills to impress the Parisian public.

'...Listen, I loved the salto precisely because it was dangerous, I wanted to do it all the time. I didn't need to be pushed into it.'

'...Without any warm-up? That was dreadfully risky!'

'...For me, that episode showed above all what little regard France had for Romania. Can you send me what you've written today? I'll call you back tomorrow. Thanks.'

How old is she?

They have to face facts: the French haven't sent anybody to welcome them at the airport. Béla and the girls have been stuck in the arrivals hall at Orly for almost an hour, he doesn't speak either French or English and doesn't understand any of the announcements being played over the loudspeakers. He only has an address written on a scrap of paper, and the gala is about to start.

According to Dorina, the taxi travels down roads that 'don't really look like Paris', and this suburban gym that they pull up outside is in a deserted street. They are greeted warmly, a woman in a navy-blue suit offers orange juice and holds out a plate of biscuits for the girls that a bemused Béla refuses. Biscuits for gymnasts! They are led to a changing room that stinks of stale cigarettes. When the hostess sees the little girls ready to perform, in their white costumes and their hair done up in bunches with red ribbons, she leans towards Nadia and starts squawking as if the girl were an irresistible little kitten. In the hall, to pre-recorded music, plump adolescent girls turn clumsy cartwheels in front of fawning parents who are clapping against the rhythm of the music.

Béla must have got the gym and the date wrong. For God's sake, let someone tell him it's a mistake, a dreadful misunderstanding; he intercepts a man in a tracksuit, points towards the French girls whose flabby thighs rub against each other as they run like blind ducks towards the vault, and then at Nadia and

Dorina, 'They real champions', he repeats. The Frenchman pats Nadia on the head. 'Yes, yes, champions one day, of course; they're so funny with their bunches.'

They are about to make their entrance when Béla, who has finally found an interpreter, realizes that the French Gymnastics Federation has sent them to an amateur exhibition and not to the event they were supposed to appear at. Anger churns his stomach: this capital bloated on ignorance, with its filthy streets and fat children; at twelve in France they can't do anything! A country that offers a paper plate filled with soft, mass-produced biscuits to his precious squirrels, what disdain!

He is pouring with sweat, he has had to run to find a taxi, but Béla has succeeded in discovering the address of the official event and managed to persuade the interpreter to accompany them. The little girls are delighted, it's a day full of adventure, they're still wearing their leotards under their tracksuits.

'No, no, no children here, only very high-level gymnasts.' The two security men bar their way into the Palais des Sports. The interpreter insists, she points at Nadia: 'a champion!', but they laugh in her face. Béla smiles politely at them and orders the girls to be ready. He steps forward, sways to and fro in front of the men like a drunken boxer, waving his arms in the air, the girls have only to crouch down and rush towards the sports hall. Pursued by the two guards, Béla also runs down gloomy corridors, shouting encouragement to Nadia in front of him, Go on, go on, straight ahead; she runs past some bewildered firemen, followed by Dorina.

On the far side of the swing door she finally pushes open, the huge, damp hall is echoing to flashes, ovations and tangos: Ludmilla has just finished her floor exercise. Nadia takes her tracksuit bottoms off as quickly as she can, it might be her turn soon and she needs to warm up. She has hardly begun when Béla rushes in, restrained by one of the guards. Scarlet-faced, he shouts at her to get out into the arena; she protests but he gesticulates at her, frowning. 'Now!'

She has not been announced. She is not wearing a number. She has not had the time to stretch her muscles. Which apparatus should she head for? The bars? The beam? No, that's impossible, another gymnast is performing there. The only free one is the vault.

Timidly, she puts one foot on the performance area. The judges and photographers turn their backs on her, all of them concentrating on a young German girl who has just entered the arena. The vault is directly in front of Nadia. The springboard is slightly twisted to the right from the weight of the previous gymnast. Nadia has no one to help her reposition it. The German girl salutes the judges. Nadia glances at Béla, who is surrounded by policemen. He encourages her, shouts, 'Go on, baby, kill them! Show them your Tsukahara!'

A confused whispering in the hall, laughter: the German girl has taken several steps backwards, knocked out of her stride by the child who has just appeared in front of her to salute the judges. She takes a deep breath, but already an official is advancing towards her, signalling for her to clear off. There's no time. Run. Run as hard as possible, build up speed, 24 kilometres an hour, leap feet together on the springboard, her hands come into brutal contact with the leather of the apparatus, a force of 180 to 270 kg/cm^2, a back handspring, the ligament in her insufficiently prepared left wrist is yanked violently, she launches into a one-and-a-half reverse pike, she has to, has to, has to. She barely closes her eyes at the shock, her dismount is perfect and the spectators buoy the air with their enthusiasm, rise spontaneously to their feet. Stupefied, for an instant the chair of judges does not react. This slender, keen body. A skill only male gymnasts can perform.

She hardly has time to get together with the other judges before a huge fellow rushes up to them, held by two guards and pursued by the Soviet coach, who is protesting vociferously.

'Madame,' pants the man, who smells of lavender and sweat, his hands pressed together, his face purple, 'Madame, I beg you, may God grant you a very long life, announce her, tell everyone her name. I beg you.'

The interpreter tries to calm one of the organizers in a dark blue suit who is growling furiously, 'This isn't a kindergarten,' looking for the little Romanian girl, but she has vanished into thin air and everybody in the stands is clapping, acclaiming the missing child. Who suddenly reappears out of nowhere, a white elf leaping onto the beam, leaving a Soviet gymnast standing there, open-mouthed.

Who is he? Her father? An uncle? This fellow the guards can hardly control because he won't stop struggling, but Béla will not let go of the judge's hand, he clasps it to his heart as he begs her, out of breath: 'Announce. Her. Name. Madame. Her name.' 'But how old is she?' asks the judge. And the answer, this twelve, makes her shudder, have they just been watching a twelve-year-old kid?

Nobody will be able to describe what Nadia accomplishes that day; all that is left are the limits of the words one has to describe something that one has never imagined.

Can one say that she grabs hold of time? Or that she takes over the air? Or that she suggests to movement that it do as she wishes? That afternoon, the exasperated organizers of the demonstration finally allow Dorina and Nadia to perform their floor exercises. It is as though they were watching the hand of a giant clock, a cursor, moving and rendering obsolete the beginnings of curves poorly contained by the leotards on the budding chests of the young women present.

A contract to disobey

While they are waiting for their plane at Orly, Béla observes the girls. They sit gaping at their surroundings, as if weighed down by the novelty, the bombardment of possibilities: a Donald Duck T-shirt on a passing teenager, the shiny scarlet lips on the pouting mouth of a model on a Rosy poster, a special offer of translucent green 'Granny Smith'-flavoured sweets, the flower-embroidered pair of jeans a young man is wearing.

Their hotel is in Montrouge, where the girls drag him into a store and methodically explore every shelf in Prisunic. Dozens of different washing powders – they come to a halt in front of the ones promising a toy in the packet – twin-coloured sponges, Coach: that one is so nice! The notebooks with bright, glossy covers, packets of toasted bread, they nod at Béla's explanations, try to imagine the taste of these dry, shrivelled pieces of bread. And these funny boxes with a transparent window on the front, just look! You can see the pasta inside! Coach, do you think we could just have the box, it's so pretty! In the end, he gives them each a coin they can put in the red distributor with the silver handle standing at the store exit. The big orange, green, yellow balls, like marbles! They all want the pink one, that one. We understand, madame, they all murmur respectfully to the assistant who warns them they can't choose the colour of the chewing gum that comes out at random. The red velvet curtains of the photo booth fascinate them, Everything here is automatic, they gush excitedly, it's so modern!

It takes Béla time to get them readjusted to their life, the one he has created for them ever since they were six. The stacks of timetables, the never-varying diet, the gestures and smells. And their calm submission to all these restrictions in the knowledge that every speck of desire, every possible deviation, a Saturday when they go for a stroll or play in their bedrooms, or have too much for tea, any one of these detours could dump them back in another life, the one ordinary children have, with no goal or future.

Nadia C. doesn't comment, but the next day when I ask her about the gymnasts' unswerving obedience, she seems troubled by the word. 'It's a contract you make with yourself, not submission to a coach. As for me, I considered the other girls, the ones who weren't gymnasts, as the obedient ones. They turned into their mothers, like all the others. We didn't.' Then she tells me what follows. I consider it anecdotal, she insists I integrate it into my account. 'It answers your question.'

For the past three months they have all been boarders at the school, even Nadia, who lives in Onești, because that way they can save a considerable amount of time without all the to-ing and fro-ing. It is past eleven at night, and they are playing in the dormitory. When they hear Béla coming, they quickly switch off the light and pretend they are asleep. He enters, switches the light back on. 'You must have made a mistake, Coach, our light is out, Coach' – but they can't help laughing beneath their blankets, excited by this fleeting moment of complicity.

'You're not sleepy? Then we'll have to tire you out a bit so that you can sleep well,' he says. 'Come on.' He doesn't even give them time to get dressed properly – 'Up you get, come on' – there they are, sockless feet in their gym shoes, delighted at the idea of this nocturnal day, laces undone, in their pyjamas in the schoolyard. He claps as he does every morning, they trot round in a circle to warm up. They laugh and point at each other, dishevelled, their cotton trousers falling down, they hold them up with both hands, Béla shouts, 'Now the jumps. Come on!' He takes them back to the dormitory past midnight, still smiling.

The next morning, the alarm goes off at five. Heads heavy, calves stiffened by the training session with no stretching, not having had the chance to drink the water they need, they take turns on the bars, the beam. Fatigue brings their hearts into their mouths. The thing they thought they had dealt with, but which reappears suddenly the moment they grasp the bars, the forbidden images, the twisted knee, torn ligaments, the thud of bones against the beam, skull, vertebrae, terror leaves their mouths dry. At nightfall, they switch off the light without a word to each other, painfully forced back into their mistreated, unwilling bodies.

Washing away their doubts

Sometimes, Stefania watches her playing outside, running around with her brother, and these normal moments don't suit Nadia, this childlike disguise superimposed on a rare piece of machinery. Nadia is always on time. Clears the table. Washes her underwear herself on her trips away, and brings it back clean. Has never uttered the kind of childish remarks Stefania could relay to her husband with delight. Even the fact that Nadia herself decides to be a boarder (the fewest steps possible, the fewest gestures apart from those she fails with in her dreams, but only in dreams) is a rational decision.

On Sundays, she demands they stretch her muscles: she clings on to the sideboard in the living room while Stefania gradually raises her daughter's leg – 'I'm not hurting you, am I?' – and the little girl impatiently orders her to lift her stupid leg up to her nose. Nadia is thirteen, looks ten, and soon none of this will interest her any more, but at least, her father asserts, the exercises are strengthening her back and her character.

The other day a photographer from *Scînteia*, the national daily newspaper, came to photograph her medals for a story. He searched a long while for the best angle, until Stefania offered to bring them all out and spread them on a nice red velvet cloth. When she asked what he was going to write in his article, he corrected her, it would only be a few lines beneath a photo of the medals: 'There's not a lot to say about little brats who know nothing of life!' Relieved, she agreed with him.

This good little girl. Who boards the train for Bucharest with Márta at the Party's invitation to attend a ceremony where for the first time she sees close up the person who looks more like a king from a movie than a comrade. Nadia is representing her team, and wears trousers and a jacket her mother has made, cobalt blue decorated with red piping at the cuffs.

Bigger than the Oneşti gym, the hall is filled with adults who clap in a much more organized way than the spectators at competitions. Perfectly synchronized, none of the sounds from their hands is misplaced. As for the Comrade, he looks older than in the portraits displayed all over the city, and his wife Elena reminds Nadia of her maths teacher, greying chignon scraped high on her head and a thick waist. The speeches go on and on. Then a little girl in traditional costume, embroidered blouse and red and white skirt, approaches the microphone.

Up to this moment, for Nadia words have been tools, useful to ask, to get or to thank. Now words swirl around in the air, vaporous sounds emerging from the mouth of this blonde girl, strips of cloud, triumphal skies and competing stars, fields of solidarity, all of them drawing a picture of her country, Romania, recited by this little child with the marvellously blue eyes. All your doubts are washed away in the radiance of this uniformly bright being: skin, hair, candyfloss voice. Faced with all this brilliance, Nadia feels dark: her hair is dark brown, her skin swarthy, Oneşti's streets are dirtied by the smoke from the factory, in its parks you won't find any of the flowers that the chosen one is offering Comrade Elena.

It's her turn. Márta pushes her forward. Confused, Nadia stands up and walks towards the podium. Is she supposed to salute them? Are they judges who will give her a score? Or spectators she should seduce? She stumbles on the step; a military man adjusts the microphone for her. And everything falls into place. The sit-ups every morning when she wakes up, before anyone, even her parents, is awake in the town, the falls, the sprains, the acrid smell of chalk she feels in her throat when she goes to bed, every piece of this dream they are celebrating together now and which she wants to participate in a lot more still, oh, she would love to be its figurehead even if she doesn't know how to recite words like the limpid girl with the blue eyes. And that takes her breath away, it rises from her stomach, the same sensation as in those milliseconds when, as she is performing a somersault, her body stupefies her and finds the floor again all on its own. The hall is on its feet applauding her, some serious-looking old people are repeating RO-MA-NI-A at the tops of their voices, she turns towards Him, what should she call him, it's Him, that's all, he has got up from his throne, is coming towards her, his eyes are more deep-set than on the portraits and it's almost as though he is going to cry, she has never seen a man cry. Does He murmur for her to step forward, or does she understand that is what she should do? He kisses her on the forehead, she promises that the Oneşti team will obtain 'the best possible results'. At the start of the year 1975, chanting rises from every smile in the hall. They are chanting the future.

Béla listens to Nadia tell him about Bucharest. Bravo, sweetheart, what a load of horseshit, all those promises you made to the Old Man, and those poems. How is she going to win anything, when he has just received a rejection letter from the Romanian Federation? None of the Oneşti gymnasts has been chosen to go to the European Championships in Norway. The girls representing Romania all come from the Dinamo Bucharest club, where the gymnasium is brand new, where the obedient young coaches every night write detailed reports on whatever might interest the Securitate: the girls they are training, the parents of the girls they are training, the jokes they share in the changing rooms. It all contributes to the Comrade's Great Construction. But what can he, Béla, offer them? Whisky, coffee, hams, Austrian chocolates smuggled across the Hungarian border, peasant gifts. And what does he receive in exchange? Nothing. Whereas his squirrels have been winning almost every competition for the past year, and will soon crush the Soviets, he's sure of it: because Olga may stand upright on the uneven bar and yes she can turn two somersaults on the beam, but she is still prone to error. She snivels, trembles. There is none of that with Nadia. Nadia on Monday is the same as Nadia on Thursday is the same as Nadia in the morning is the same as Nadia in the evening. What more do they want? What needs to be improved? Even Nadia's parents are exemplary. Discreet. Keep out of politics. Romanians to be proud of, solid, like their own grandparents, an eternity of modest trustworthiness.

Béla travelled to Bucharest without an appointment. He asked to see the man from the Ministry of Sport. No luck. He returned to Oneşti, no one can replace him for the training sessions, then left again for the capital to try once more. Nothing doing, nobody would see him. On the telephone, he begs an official to find a solution, careful not to contradict this 'excellent national decision', but please, please can they not add one gymnast to the team, just one of his girls? He can hardly boast of his triumph in Paris because that adventure was frowned upon, the details of it reaching the Federation executives thanks to the Parisian interpreter, a young Securitate recruit. The French have made an official complaint. In their own style, of course, politely, expressing astonishment at 'the surprise presentation of those marvellous young Romanian girls who were not part of the programme'.

Comrade, the official who finally receives him in Bucharest tells him, Your girls have time, they are barely thirteen! What a joke, he chortles to his colleagues as soon as Béla leaves his office, that Hungarian imagines our modern, progressive country could be represented by some dwarf peasants from a town of retards in the arsehole of the east of the country!

Is there another meeting that Béla keeps secret? Or does he in the end have more high-placed friends than he is willing to admit? Does he find better gifts? Promise a gold medal, a title? A week later, he is finally given permission to add one of his girls to the Romanian national team. So there will be three from Dinamo and one from Oneşti.

Too old to be young

Twenty-five seconds into her routine on the beam at Skien, in Norway, her wrists undulate in air that seems solid, feet together on the ten centimetres of wood, an incongruous movement of her hips to right and left, a little girl miming an imaginary rock 'n' roll, Nadia reaches out with her hands and without touching the beam performs a rapid sweep with her legs, the white knot on her ponytail acting as a reference point: 'You are here.' She climbs so high when she does the swing movement that some of the audience cannot watch the exercise to the end, terrified her thin arms will give way and she will fall. Does she know, is she aware that she could break her neck, worried journalists ask the dazzled judges. In a red tracksuit on the second step of the podium, Ludmilla Tourischeva watches the child just crowned the youngest ever European champion salute the public. Her face looks tense, there is a sweetly sad bitterness to her smile. Faded.

I write to Nadia C., 'Your grand entrance is a spectacle whose perfect choreography is based on twin-coloured accessories, white and red. The white of the virginal leotard. The white of the chalk, from the palm of your hands to your thighs. And the androgynous pallor of the young girl gymnasts before it was decided, at the beginning of the nineties, to paint them with make-up and sparkly eyeliner that would be more commercial. And red. The red of communism

and its flags, of course. But above all the red satin of the outland-
ish bows the coaches decorated your hair with, that accessory as a
guarantee of childhood in a world where you were always "too old
to be young".'

If it doesn't bleed

European champion! The news is such a surprise that they can't even find a photo to illustrate the story that appears on the morning of her return to Bucharest. At the airport, arms piled high with red carnations, they are waiting for her, the one who has just dethroned the Soviets. A young woman finally emerges from the plane, wearing a navy-blue tracksuit. It's NA-DI-A! Oh, isn't she beautiful! But bizarrely, a huge moustachioed man hands her some plastic bags and then clasps a little girl by the shoulder, she must be his daughter. Where is our great athlete? enquires an official, looking for the outline of a powerful sportswoman. Then the little girl, Nadia, steps towards them, her medals forming a strange tribal necklace, a gold breastplate on her narrow chest, and almost in slow motion the photographers kneel down to be level with the child's pale face.

Nadia shakes hands. A Party representative thanks her in the name of the entire country for having kept her word, for having achieved the good results she had promised Comrade Ceaușescu.

Everything that happens during the rest of 1975 – if one wanted to make up the story from scratch, one wouldn't know where to start – the painstaking, exemplary climb to fame, is seen by Béla as nothing more than a confirmation. He was right. Nadia assuages his doubts, anticipates his fears, complies with every-thing, the ambassador of his dream, the subject of an experiment in which she is the Nearly Princess. Nearly. Because now he has to convince the authorities to make room for the girls from Oneşti in the future Olympic team.

Béla swears that his little girls will smash the Russians, look, he writes it in ink and signs it on the paper napkin of the restaurant where he has invited three members of the Federation: Comrades, if you take my girls, after Montreal no one will remember the Soviets!

This big fat guy makes them laugh, he is almost touching when he strikes up the Romanian national anthem, on his feet and keeping time with his hand as though leading troops: 'Today, the Party unites us and on the soil of Romania socialism is being built by the efforts of the workers for the honour of the fatherland, we are crushing our enemies so that we can live with dignity under the sun among the other peoples, in peace, in pea-eace.'

All right, so there will be a preliminary competition between the two teams, the decision will be made according to results, the members of the Federation concede, amused at the spectacle created by the man they continue to call the Hungarian.

Summer in the capital, the fragrance of linden trees clinging to the concrete. The heat hangs from you like burning hooks, the air seems to solidify, stagnant and damp. Here, in the vast glassed-in gymnasium, there are no old mattresses strewn on the floor, but electric blue rubber mats. When the temperature soars above thirty-eight degrees, the Dinamo club coaches who insist their gymnasts call them 'Comrade Coach' take them to Constanța on the Black Sea. The girls from Oneşti drag themselves to the washroom between exercises, splash cold water on their faces.

Is it Béla who has suggested the Federation send someone that day? This general in charge of sports who enters the gymnasium and signals to Béla to continue the training while he sits down? Béla is over the moon. It couldn't have come at a better moment. What does it matter that Luminița complains she has a migraine (Get back up on the beam, when you jump they can hear you as far away as Transylvania, you're as graceful as a cow, come on, you can afford to lose a few grams of sweat), or that Dorina collapses four times on the run while attempting a double back somersault? The general will soon grow tired of the smell of sweat mixed with chalk that makes the atmosphere even drier. There is no need for Béla to do anything but wait for him to stand up, dust off his uniform and come over to ask, 'Where are the gymnasts from the Dinamo club, Comrade Professor?' To which he will reply innocently that they are 'at the beach, as usual when the sun is shining'. The general leaves in a fury and orders to see the two teams' representatives. The next day, the Dinamo coach excuses himself by claiming 'the young girls need to rest in this heat'. Béla raises his eyebrows. 'What's that? Rest? Is rest part of the Olympic programme?' The general appoints him director of the national and Olympic teams; Béla is the one who will choose the gymnasts.

Done. Everything has to be perfect. He instructs Márta to find a new doctor they can trust; this one from Bucharest doesn't understand a thing about gymnastics, he's impossible, the way he purses his lips disapprovingly, his paternalistic advice. The squirrels bounce back, get carried away, their backs bend double. If it doesn't bleed, Béla assures the little girls, don't worry, it's probably nothing very serious.

Biomechanics of a Communist fairy

15 November 1975

In 1975, the National Visa and Passport Commission was a department of the Securitate. Its name was nothing more than a decoy, since hardly any passports were given apart from to Party high-ups. In reality, this commission was there to identify those who wanted to leave the country and were asking for a visa. They were immediately sacked from their jobs and put under special surveillance.

For their pre-Olympic tour, the Romanian gymnastics team is travelling to Germany and the United States, then Canada and even Japan. From 1975 on, is Nadia a simple Romanian citizen, or is she a piece of the flag, a story being written, a national weapon? She who cannot even recall, she tells me, having learned the regulations of the competitions she takes part in, as if the scoring systems were born at the same time as her and guaranteed her progress. Small, invisible crosses drawn on her path to show her where to place her feet.

He hangs up. Sits on his bed, strangely tired, almost dazed. Béla would like to listen again to the words spoken by this fellow from the Federation who has just informed him about the telegram from London. Perhaps he misunderstood. He dials the Bucharest number again.

'Excuse me, Comrade Bălcescu... Is it sportswoman of the

year, or gymnast of the year?' If it is what he first thought, gymnast of the year, it's only a grudging recognition, almost an imitation title offered to a prissy little madam performing sugary steps. Something that would take no account of the twenty-seven kilometres an hour run-up to the vault they measured the previous week. But rather than encourage him, this title of sportswoman of the year becomes a concern. Like a future promise he is not sure he can keep. Márta and he have created the European champion without following any real recipe. They have to reinforce the possible. If they succeed in reducing the percentage of the unknown, of chance, in Nadia, they are bound to secure even better results.

Everything she puts in her mouth is calculated time and again. A hundred grams of meat at midday, and fifty in the evening, that comes to about four hundred calories, vegetables with her meals, two hundred grams each: a hundred and twenty calories. Three yogurts a day: a hundred and eighty. And fruit, perhaps three pieces a day: a hundred and fifty calories. No bread, starch or sugar, obviously. Think about drawing a line on the bottle of oil Silvina the cook uses; if it's more than the stipulated fifty millimetres a day, all their calculations will be out. He has already had many arguments with Silvina, but to argue isn't to decide. He will supervise the menus himself.

He redesigns their daily timetables: 6–8 in the morning, training; 8–12, school; 12–13, meal; 13–14, rest; 14–16, classes; 16–21, training; 21–22, dinner, lessons and bedtime. He changes doctors again until he finds one who never questions any of his decisions. The child's blood is pored over, her breathing measured, urine transformed into a biological formula. Every morning prior to training she undergoes tests of strength: sets of knee bends and push-ups. He machines her abdominal muscles into steel sheathing so that she won't grimace the moment her hips crash into the uneven bar, her bones barely protected by the blue fabric. Her strength has to be built up to take account of the unforeseen: fatigue, a chill. Béla reads biology treatises, underlines whole passages, meets athletics coaches: what do you do to make them run faster? I make them run farther, the guy replies. So he increases the repetitions of their routines. Until now, they have been doing them ten times a day, and then concentrating on the details. The new figure is fixed arbitrarily: twenty-five times in the morning, and twenty-five in the afternoon.

For the first few months, none of them has the strength in their muscles to perform more than fifteen times the minute and a half of somersaults, balancing and saltos. They stumble, their tetanized muscles make them stagger from one exercise to the next like panting drunkards. The whole day he orders: Do it again. Start again. Their wrists give way under their weight when they try to balance. Cramps keep them awake at night, hunger wakens them earlier and earlier, at four in the morning he hears them whispering in the dormitory. At dinner, they feed themselves silently, mechanically raising forks to their mouths. Their tears change as well: what they cry over at each training session is the impossibility of going farther, furious at this edifice of tendons and muscles that yield before they do.

Béla works with intoxication, giddiness. He has a pit built round the bars and the beam that is filled with big chunks of thick foam. He encourages his girls to run and throw themselves into it. Each day he adds an extra exercise to their run until they lose completely their fear of falling, their arched backs disdainful of the floor. And everything accelerates, their voices become shriller, their leaps are more rapid, all fear is blunted. Each evening, they line up to see the doctor for repairs. Strained or twisted muscles they beg him to make disappear by the next morning. The doctor does his best to comply. Offers anti-inflammatories, painkillers and cortisone. At Christmas, they go home for three days' holiday.

Play madly

On 27 December Stefania accompanies Nadia back to the boarding school and watches a training session. She would like to cover her eyes when the gymnasts explore the horizon with a leap, invert floor and ceiling, make the air elastic. Her daughter starts again. Climbs back onto the beam. Falls off. Breathless, she grabs a bowl and barely swallows a mouthful before she tries another double back somersault. At four in the afternoon, on a signal from Béla, the gym is emptied, the cleaner is sent home together with the other coaches and even the pianist. The only ones left are Nadia, Béla and Stefania, whom Béla makes promise she won't breathe a word of what she is about to witness. The curtains are drawn, the lights are switched on in broad daylight.

It is as if she is no longer there. The child seems transfixed by a mission whose name she herself is unaware of. Not a single glance towards her mother or him. Her pale, strained face, lips pressed tight shut, lines under her eyes, she takes a deep breath and nods to Béla, who lifts her and raises her directly to the higher bar. She starts the necessary swing movement, gathering speed. Then, at a signal from Béla, she lets go and spins head over heels between the bars, her thighs spread out wide, the back of her neck brushes against the wood, she just manages to recover.

This surprise move is a secret, a declaration of world dominance no one as yet knows about. This unimaginable leap, for which all thought of broken bones, torn tendons or cracked vertebrae has to be put aside. For which she has to play madly, outside the rules. This unimaginable salto which has arisen from a mistake one morning several months earlier.

That day, Nadia is preparing to execute a classic somersault from a support position. Is it her body that, in order not to perish, seeks a way of escape just at the moment when her hands slip and she misses the bar, her pelvis violently striking the wood? Béla leaps towards her but too late, and anyway, if she… it will always be too late. She manages to grab hold of the bar she has just let go of. He suggests a glass of lemonade, a break, she refuses, she is very pale, as if she is about to throw up, then thinks better of it, disoriented, stunned but also extremely excited because she didn't fall off. The two of them are quiet.

Which of them succeeds in rediscovering and unravelling what has happened, to make a fair copy of it? Possibly it is not him who dares propose they retrace the steps of the narrowly avoided fall, but her? From the next day on, Béla and the girl set to work to tame their marvellous mistake.

Gymnastic manoeuvres are classified according to their degree of difficulty. A figure A is considered simple, B is more complicated. Level E is only attempted by a very few girls in the world. Let's say, sweetheart, we'll call that a Super-E! When he sends the IOC the skills his gymnasts are going to perform at Montreal, Béla doesn't mention any Es, still less a Super-E. After all, at Munich the Soviets had caught all the other countries out by 'forgetting' to describe the skills in Olga K.'s programme.

'In 1972 the International Gymnastics Federation grew alarmed at the "dangerous figures performed by Olga K. that could lead to a fractured pelvis". It was considered they should be banned. In 1976, Károlyi was asked if what you performed didn't place you in great danger. "That's possible," he replied, "but Nadia never falls."'

She sighs. Falls silent. 'Are there things you don't like in the chapter?' I ask nervously.

Nadia: 'No... But I can see what you're driving at... Sport in eastern Europe and the dreadful methods employed, etc.' I start to protest, but she interrupts me. 'Give me your postal address, please.'

A few days later I receive an envelope. Inside it is a copy of an article published in 1979 in the bulletin of the French Gymnastics Federation. The officials are worried about the retransmission of the European Championships in Strasbourg showing the gymnasts' numerous serious falls, because 'they give a poor image of our sport'. The TV channel agrees to 'place less emphasis' on these incidents in the broadcasting of upcoming competitions.

A chalk Joan of Arc

26 March 1976, Madison Square Garden, New York

How to describe a young girl who reels off danger like so many nursery rhymes she soon becomes bored with? The chair of judges tots up her score again, unable to believe her eyes. She looks for mistakes so that she can deduct a few tenths of a point, but there's nothing. It's 10. In Japan the following week, at the Chunichi Cup, two more 10s, for the bars and vault.

Béla keeps a close watch on the lines under her eyes, her breath: is she drinking enough between training sessions? He also has to look after the others, who are now the ornaments, the walk-ons: the other girls in the team. Boring, predictable, with the fear and fatigue they try to conceal, whereas Nadia is a danger-eating carnivorous plant who can never get enough. She follows the dictates of her body, which is capable of tracing fire in the air, a chalk Joan of Arc. She gnaws at the impossible, then lays it aside to move on to the next, always the next.

'Ye-es. Reading you, right from the start you describe Béla as a kind of... specialist, whereas he didn't know very much at all!'

'He showed you the skills, he must have known something, mustn't he?'

'He learned gymnastics at the same time as I did.' (She laughs,

but since I can't see her I'm unable to tell whether she's really amused or being sarcastic.)

According to her, Béla was a kind of inspired manager, a visionary rather than a technician, with, as during the Paris meet, ideas that 'would make her visible to western Europe'.

'What about Geza, the choreographer of your marvellous floor exercise at Montreal, that was truly inspired! That mixture of childish gestures and acrobatics, that humour...'

'Geza... yes, he knew how to observe me in my real life and he could sense what would please the judges. He was a kind of... manager.'

'Goodness! So many managers! Because, in a sense, Ceaușescu himself "managed" your image...'

'Yes, they were all managers. A lot of managers. A lot.'

Yes, Sir, That's My Baby

For Nadia, Geza first develops a choreography highlighting her suppleness and speed to a military march in four-four time. Béla and Márta reject it. In his second version, to an air from *Scheherazade*, he instructs her to increase the languid droop of her wrists, to make her pelvis flexible and to work on the oriental tilt of her head. Geza doesn't even need to wait for Nadia to finish to realize his mistake. Trying desperately to appear sensual, the little girl barely wiggles her hips and only looks lopsided. She casts almost embarrassed glances at them, as if all she wants is to go and put her clothes on. They thank her, send her off for a shower and to bed.

For a moment Béla says nothing, they are on their own in the gym, then, well-nigh incoherent with rage, he accuses Geza of wanting to sabotage Nadia with his crap, you make me sick, and when Geza threatens to pull out there and then, he begs him to find something else, anything rather than having to keep those horrors, I'm sorry, Geza, I need you, so much, so much, I want something tailor-made for Nadia at Montreal, something really, really new! Still clasping his cigarette, he tries out a few steps, singing to himself, Like this, you see, perhaps in this style, a heavy transvestite mimicking childhood, 'something light, enchanting, tralala'.

Friends again, the two men go in search of salami and tomatoes in the kitchen and, sitting at the big Formica table, review the competition. The Soviets of Ludmilla's generation, coached by Bolshoi ballet dancers, who slip a desolate *port de bras* or two into some perfect acrobatics to an air by Tchaikosvky, that's old hat. They need to look instead at what Olga does. Olga who, in Munich, tied ribbons in her hair. She wrinkles up her nose like a comical hamster, simpers before launching into a skill (E) which, if she messes it up, will break her neck; with her, intensity and drama have become old fashioned. Olga, miming a memory of childhood she won't let go of, because, as Béla remarks, she will soon be twenty-one.

And Nadia, what is there to say about Nadia? It's true she fascinates thanks to her technique, she excels at that. But how long will it take the Russians to find one similar, a Super-E? A few months? And if you had only three adjectives to describe her, what would you say about Nadia? Serious-perfect-imperturbable? Impeccable-precise-impressive? What she needs is a 'trick', something fucking big, really special, like a signature, you see? Something simple, they tell each other, by now completely drunk. But none of those stupid tricks for fat old ladies, eh, you're not going to dirty my smooth-cheeked squirrel, Béla insists, laughing when they finally say goodnight, and Geza goes to bed without a single fresh idea apart from one certainty: it is embarrassing to see Nadia wiggle her hips. It's embarrassing, ridiculous, to see Nadia waving her arms coquettishly through the air: she needs to be seen climbing a tree or running along a beach, opening Christmas presents and clapping her hands, Nadia is the age the others are pretending to be, flimsily disguised as little girls, trying to ward off the very unsporting desire they arouse, their chests emphasized by the elastic fabric.

Geza searches. For weeks he experiments. Nadia skimps on her schooling and her rest periods. They try different types of music, cast them off like unsuitable garments, no, those folk songs and waltzes are just too hackneyed. Dan the pianist rummages in his bag, comes up with a tune a friend has brought back from abroad: 'Young Americans' by David Bowie. What if the judges thought this was too risqué? Another no. That afternoon they spend hours getting nowhere, Dan has a cigarette in his left hand, while with his free hand, almost as an afterthought, to relax a bit, he plays the tune 'Yes, Sir, That's My Baby', a charleston from 1925. Nadia, who for lunch is drinking some lemonade, is sitting cross-legged on the big floor mat that is so threadbare in parts it's hard to see the white line marking the performance square. She starts nodding her head to the rhythm, then stands up in front of the pianist and to amuse him begins to make exaggeratedly jerky gestures as if she is in a silent film. She advances towards Béla, stamping her heels on the floor, arms swinging. She is quite funny, far more than she usually allows herself to be with them, she is playacting to lighten the atmosphere, but above all, Geza thinks dreamily as he watches her, she is adorable. Unbearably cute. You feel like pinching her cheek, slapping her bottom and sending her out to perform again, and again. From that moment on, he composes with her as the starting point. He re-engineers very little of what she does. There's not much for him to adjust, she has got it already. Once the 'fussy stuff' – that's what Béla calls the dance steps – are out of the way, he sprinkles the choreography with acrobatic skills that as yet have no name, invents what he dreams for her at the same time as he instructs her on the movements he requires; she succeeds in doing what no one ever dared think she would accept.

She falls. Flat on her back/her front/almost on her head, and one morning he rushes over to her, frightened she might have concussion. The speed with which she escapes from his arms and holds out her hands for him to lift her up again… They bind up her ankles. Her Achilles tendon is swollen, an excrescence protected by foam held in place with Scotch tape, the stigmata from the number of times she has struck the lower bar with her foot. Her knees fill with liquid as a reaction to all the repeated shocks, her joints are covered with patches of hard skin. They have to be careful that the open blisters on her hands don't get infected by dust from the floor or the chalk. Her body–weight ratio is so perfect that when she runs to leap into backward tumbles you can't quite believe her feet are even touching the ground. Dan complains that Nadia is always getting ahead of the music in her first diagonal. Follow her, he is told. Stay with her. As the games draw nearer, no one from outside is allowed into the gym; the doors are locked. They invent names for the newly invented skills, the Super-E is baptized the 'Comăneci salto', a birth celebrated officially at an impromptu party at Béla's place, where he gives Nadia a new doll for her collection.

'I'm not calling too late am I, Nadia?'

'No, it's OK. I'm sorry, but I haven't had time to read the most recent pages.'

'Don't worry. Look, I saw a documentary yesterday. The commentator says this, and I quote: "At the Olympic Games in Mexico in 1968, it's true Věra Čáslavská was a very beautiful woman, but one never had the impression she could hurt herself if she fell." Whereas at Munich in 1972, Olga gave him goosebumps because she was so pretty and so young and because for the first time ever in a gym, people were frightened. For her, for her life. To hear veteran journalists getting excited by danger makes me think… is it a must to have little girls flirting with an accident? There's something… pornographic… about it… And… hello, are you still there? Do you think I'm exaggerating?'

'…No. Let's talk about it later. About the risk. As soon as you've got beyond my childhood. I wish you a very good night.'

Managers in the East
(the coming of the red ribbons)

Do managers always think in these terms? That it's a good idea to decorate the story they are telling with add-ons, like Věra Čáslavská's hairstyle? Hair like a rock 'n' roll princess, backcombed into a tall bouffant kept in place by a black band that matches her eyeliner, an after-dark American hairstyle. Irresistibly superior, Véra performs skills only men can do. A spotless white Peter Pan collar sets off the black of her costume, her pointed breasts don't tremble when she bends forward, she could almost hold a champagne glass in her hand as she collects the gold and silver with a smile.

Véra is a witch in a Peter Pan collar. Véra is deliciously dangerous. Her voice rang out loud and clear during the Prague Spring, when she demonstrated against the Soviet invasion and signed the two-thousand-word manifesto. Véra is a muscular fairy. In her hideaway in a Moravian forest where she goes to ground, harassed by the new powers in place, she trains all alone with a fallen tree trunk for a balancing beam. But the Olympic Games are approaching and they can't do without her, so she is invited to leave her forest, all is forgiven…

When the Czech team enters the stadium for the opening ceremony in Mexico, the crowd gets carried away and chants: 'Free-dom Czech-o-slov-akia Vé-ra' as she marches past. Véra makes short work of the competition, what an appetite she has, joyous solar cravings, her skills have been invented and practised on grass, she spins round, her hair deliciously askew, salutes the judges. The public is on its feet, elated at having seen Čáslavská's towering performance, the journalists comment on the gold medal that will surely be hers in a few moments. Unnoticed, three men in grey suits sitting not far from the judges' table go over to the Soviet Larisa Petrik to congratulate her. But not to the Czechs, whose coach takes Véra in his arms and consoles her for this last-minute demonstration of allegiance to the Soviets by the Czechoslovak apparatchiks. The two gymnasts have to share the title and the medal.

Véra straightens up. She violates the protocol she has been instructed to follow, yet again. And very few of the millions of TV viewers, so few, are able to understand the implacable message Véra sends to the Czech authorities when, at the first strains of the Soviet national anthem, she ostentatiously lowers her gaze. The daisy stuck in her blonde hair quivers slightly with her breathing. In front of the whole world's cameras, Véra turns her back on the red flag slowly being raised. Farewell, Véra.

In the West, people are very, very shocked that the gold medal has eluded her, there's no excuse for all this Olympic dishonesty. And Čáslavská's class, her courage in the face of the oppressor, will never be forgotten. Ban the USSR? The idea was put to the Committee, but that would be harmful to the sport, after all, they have such a reserve of astonishing gymnasts! The Munich games are approaching, and there is talk of an amazing surprise the Soviets have in store. Some of them claim to have seen a photograph of a very young girl who is able to hold herself upright on the top bar, the one the others can only just cling on to. It's said that in secret since 1970 the Soviets have been training her to do something no woman in the world has dared to do: a backwards somersault on the beam. Olga K. is this no-other-young-woman-in-the-world. A sharp ferret with crooked teeth, she is really amusing, she has straight, silky hair that her coach ties in bunches with ribbons. When she puts her pretty feet together, her baby frog's thighs have a gap between them, the skin on the back of her neck is golden, silk protecting her vertebrae, such sweet little bones.

O.L.G.A. Who dissolves in tears in front of the camera lenses, and accumulates stupid mistakes when she is on the uneven bars in Munich. Huddled in her chair from the realization of her failure, she wipes her nose with her hand as she waits for the scores, her face drawn, surrounded by sturdy young women, none of whom even glance her way. A Soviet girl crying! So they're not all robots! The over-emotional communist who messed up is snivelling live and in colour, to the great delight of American magazines which are wild about this so unwarlike Russian. But the very next day she recovers and delivers what was promised. Glittering moments of fear. Her slender neck that could be snapped in two when she pulls off a skill that eight years later will be banned by the judges as being too dangerous. No one even knows whether she won, and no one cares, they are all cooing with delight at this 'freshness', this cool breeze, how wonderful, 'it's as if she were seven years old!'

Montreal, 1976. Olga is twenty-one. Miraculously, the little girl is still little. Exhausted from having to fulfil all the Soviet state's demands, four years of galas and dinners, her skin looks dull from lack of sleep. They tie red ribbons in her straggly hair to gain time, to hear more of the public's thrilled sighs, mmmm. Red satin bows like the curtains in a back room where she will be offered one last time to eager eyes, red like an accessory that prolongs desire, red which confirms to the buyer the freshness of the image purchased, red the satin sheen of this garter-belt substitute, that's what is needed, red bows to gain a few more moments because the Other, the new Romanian girl, is only fourteen and is Adorable.

Numbers

'*Listen, it's funny,*' *she tells me, very excited, 'I had seven tens and won three gold medals in Montreal. That makes twenty-one, the twenty-first Olympiad, and if you add seven and three, my competition number, you again get: ten, the perfect score!*'

'*Here's another number, Nadia. Twenty thousand. Twenty thousand attempts/repetitions of the salto before performing it on the bars at Montreal, the Comăneci salto...*'

A pause at the other end of the line, during which it seems to me she is shrugging her shoulders and has become sullen once more.

'*...Of course! What else did you imagine?*'

'*...You arrived in Montreal about ten days before the competition to prepare thoroughly. You were accompanied the whole time by interpreters who rephrased everything you said. What was your relationship with the other gymnasts, those from western Europe? What did you think about the obvious differences between you, their freedom?*'

'*...You know, they were... quite bad. They didn't interest me. I knew the Russians quite well, especially Nellie, because we'd been meeting at competitions for three years. As for the other things... do you think the Romanian regime was the only one to keep an eye on its gymnasts during international meets? In gymnastics, every country tries to find out what the other will do, it's a game of chess. You're not going to give away your secrets to your opponent! We were told to tell the press we trained three hours a day, when it was* six. *That kept us one step ahead!'*

'Montreal marketed the image of an innocent little girl who came out of nowhere, whereas in fact you had been winning everything for two years. You contributed to the creation of that image. And through you, the regime promoted a system. The complete success of the communist regime, the apotheosis of selection: the exceptionally gifted New Child, a beautiful, well-behaved girl who delivers.'

(An irritated laugh.)

'Oh yes, of course! The Romanians were selling communism. Yet the French or American athletes nowadays... they don't represent any system or brand, do they?...'

Special offer

Montreal, 1976

On the table, jars filled with a brownish paste, bowls containing a lumpy white cheese, and big flat pancakes covered in tomato sauce, ham, and melted cheese. In her diary, Dorina carefully notes all these stupefying details of their Olympic stay. Never before has she seen *peanut butter, cottage cheese* or *pizzas*. The cornflakes they are served in the morning give them the giggles. 'Cereal? They eat like animals over here!' 'And did you see, Coach, how they chew all the time?' The girls discover to their amazement that Western jaws are constantly in movement, chewing gum, sandwiches, sweets, snacks.

For his part, Béla knows he has to work quickly, to fast-forward through their amazement and stupefaction. To limit the impact of the spectacle. Not point out to his charges the helicopters transporting the athletes to events for security reasons, or the controls and endless searches at the entrance gates.

On every trip to the West, Béla is careful to go directly from gym to hotel, hotel to gym, the girls scarcely have time to collect the miniature pots of jam and shampoo samples before they are whisked away in the aeroplane back to Bucharest. Here in Montreal, the bars of chocolate wrapped in silver and exclamation marks ('Guaranteed pleasure!!!') create an unavoidable, many-tentacled global carousel that never allows anyone to fully concentrate; in the Olympic village, everything appeals to the girls, who stretch a hesitant hand out to the latest Nike models exhibited in the hall, a honeyed world infiltrating them. Neither Béla nor Márta can do much to counteract the 628 sponsors jostling in the village avenues.

Yellow-costumed clowns offer the athletes miniature cans, a whole array of orange, brown or green acidic carbonated drinks, purple plastic bowls overflowing with sticks of chewing gum, sweets the colours of the games, you can plunge into piles of T-shirts in huge baskets, caps, badges, teddy bears of all sizes, Oh, can I take one for my brother, Comrade Coach? And off each of them goes with three little bears under their arm, key-rings, balls, shiny ribbons, writing paper as well. Bewildered, they stare at posters announcing 'Special Offers!!!' in the village boutiques. Three for two! A dollar off if you buy the whole set!!! 'They pay people to buy here,' says Luminiţa. In comfortable rooms with soft lighting, the latest hits (ABBA, Elton John and Kiki Dee!) drown out the sounds of the permanently switched-on television. The Romanian girls stop, grasp Márta by the arm, look, look, they say, when the jingle at the start of the adverts comes on. These mini-films are so won-der-ful, Madame Coach. And so funny… The coffee tables are piled high with magazines. They test the sofas, leaf through *Elle*, *Life*, *OK!*, but don't recognize anyone apart from… 'Alain Delon!' they shout joyously. They burst out laughing at every loud 'quack' – 'it's a duck!' – from the security machines they have to go through several times a day.

Everything's so modern, Dorina keeps repeating, so 'hi-tech', a term she learned that morning from a magazine. Hi-tech, permanent temptation, all this comfort: at breakfast, they have barely finished their fruit juice when a fragrant voice wafts over their shoulder offering them more. Hi-tech, these hundreds of hostesses deposited like healthy, shiny plants, so attentive you're sure you must already have met them somewhere, how else to explain their affectionate familiarity, the waves of the hand that accompany their 'bye-byes'. They're beautiful, beautiful beautiful, Dorina says to Nadia over and over, so modern! They smell of mint and lacquer, they're as elastic as athletes who never perspire.

In the face of this flood of possibilities, Béla is powerless. All these superfluous images, this background noise, it's all dangerous fatty tissue. In Onești, some people would say that once you've gone round the town all that's left to do is to go round it again in the opposite direction. And yet that is not really emptiness, the quiet of an open road, the space, the atmosphere that leaves room for gestures. Silence among the trees, stalls with gritty, misshapen fruit and vegetables, a few dolls in the only toy shop in town, small courtyards where children play until it grows dark, when you go home, listen to music on the radio or read for a long while before falling asleep. The confined limits of that world contain a boundless inward horizon; here, the countless offers reduce space, this Western waltz that leaves you feeling sick from too much spinning round.

'Were you impressed by all that abundance?'

'Of course. You know, the first time my mother came to the West was in a New Jersey suburb. She started crying in the aisles of the small supermarket there.'

I try to understand. Was Stefania crying tears of joy faced with the emotion of all these new choices? But Nadia interrupts me almost brutally. She was disgusted at the absurd piles of stuff, she corrects me. Sad at feeling herself tempted by desire on seeing all these heaps of nothing. 'Back home there was nothing to desire. But in the West, you are called on to desire constantly.'

We have a long talk on the telephone about what I call Béla's 'manipulations', his occasionally desperate attempts to propel into the limelight someone who is already the European champion but whom the Western media show no interest in. I send my pages to Nadia, she makes no comment, but weeks later writes to me, 'The word "manipulation" is too negative. The myth of the gymnast that the whole world discovers because she is so brilliant is completely mistaken. The judges need to have already heard of a gymnast to pay her attention and score her correctly. Béla was aware of that. When we arrived in Montreal, no one knew about us; they were all concentrating on the Russians. Béla wasn't just a coach, he was more like a coach–agent–lawyer... Write "plan", please, not "manipulation".'

Béla's manipulations or plans

He shouted, banged his fists, offered packets of Kent and promises of medals to all the officials in the Romanian Federation and the Central Committee. He slapped stupid weaklings, threw away cakes he found under dormitory beds and deprived the guilty girls of their dinner, he sacked seven doctors, forgot the names – without even meaning to – of those who were too badly injured to be there today, he took care of the budget of fifty-six *lei* (thirty pence) per child per day, Eating will lead you to your graves more quickly, my darlings. He tore small strips of skin from the palms of his hands and stuck them on Nadia's burst blisters, skin repairs skin! None of this gets him anywhere: nobody knows Romania, and not a single journalist has asked for an interview since they arrived in the Olympic village. Béla has bought all the newspapers, only switched the television off after watching the news in English and French. Not a thing, apart from a brief mention in a specialized report.

Why is this, when for the past two years Nadia has been upsetting the reigning champions, why no article, why so few photos, why is Nadia still no more than a rumour? The frustration at being held back, as if at an invisible frontier, by the Russians, who are blocking his view of the West. And in the background, his squirrel-clown.

On 17 July, the hall is only half full. The speaker announces the Romanian team to lukewarm applause from the public. They line up to make their entrance, but Béla holds Nadia back by the arm. The speaker repeats, 'The team from Romania!' Béla gestures to them not to move, while he explains to the official who comes over to hurry them up that one of his little girls is in the toilet, *sorry*. The tone of the announcement changes. 'The team from Romania?' Nadia mutters. 'It's our turn, Comrade Professor,' as if he has suffered a sudden amnesia. Béla leans down to her, whispers something in her ear, which she whispers to Dorina, who in turn whispers it to Mariana, and so on until it reaches Luminița, who claps her hands with delight.

When they finally appear, marching in perfect formation, everybody has turned towards them. What is this? A pageant? A mistake? What are such young girls – how old can they be, to look at they can't be more than twelve years old – doing here? And all dressed the same, a real army, whereas even if you are sitting far away, among the Soviets you can make out Ludmilla in pink and Nellie in royal blue. The dull white of their costumes is edged with stripes of blue–yellow–red from their thighs to under their arms. And like a target on their chests, the national emblem: conifers and mountains squeezed beneath a naive yellow sun and surrounded by ears of wheat, with a red star over hearts untroubled by any hint of breasts.

The girls from the different teams greet one another politely and begin their warm-ups, avoiding the complex skills so as not to risk any last-minute injury. Except for them. Confident of Béla's plan of attack, they hurtle from one piece of apparatus to the next, a gang of bandits who unhesitatingly perform their entire routines as though the competition had already begun.

The speaker calls an end to the warm-up session and they all return to the wings, that neutral space where opponents brush against one another without ever speaking, an unwritten law. One that the Romanian girls are busy trampling on. Joyously loutish, they invade this area of rest and waiting, they trample on the Olympic regulations: an electric bundle of nerves in the humid arena, Dorina turns a double somersault that finishes almost at the feet of an astonished Ludmilla. Not so much as glancing at the Soviet girl, she nonchalantly tightens the elastic of her bunches, humming to herself. Then it's Nadia's turn to come near Olga, two back flips one after the other, her foot catches the terrified Soviet champion's arm. The Russians press up against each other, circling round their astounded coaches, how can Béla allow his gymnasts to run the risk of stumbling on bags or tracksuits left on the floor! They are about to protest when Béla whistles and claps his hands and the little ones trot daintily towards him.

The American TV channels quickly adjust the placing of their cameras so that they can grab close-ups of the faces of the Russians, Ludmilla, Olga and Nellie, visibly upset at the message the Romanians have delivered, their belligerent explosions, skills nobody in the hall can even name.

Nowadays, the story has it that at Montreal Nadia performed to complete silence. In fact, the music for the floor exercise of one of the Russians was blaring out, while another was sprinting towards the vault to shouts of encouragement from the public. It's said that Béla rudely silenced the woman sitting next to him, who, while Nadia was dancing on the beam, begged God for it all to stop. He saw every detail, every leap and pirouette, everything, as an obstacle course to be overcome, one item after another, he stared at the left ankle strapped the previous week following a sprain, let it, oh, let it hold. Dorina remembers the moment when she was convinced Nadia could never fall, as if she no longer knew how to. Hail Nadia full of grace, stutters the commentator during the live broadcast of the exercise. And she will have to respond endlessly to this narrative, pore over the images and numbers as though they are a mystery for which she still has no answer.

When I ask her, 'Do you realize the impact you had in 1976?' Nadia replies, like someone sleepwalking through her super-childhood, 'No, I don't know, I still wonder about it… What was it I did?'

You scrubbed the future clean, and destroyed the narrow, pretty path reserved for little girls, I want to tell Nadia C., thanks to you, little girls in the summer of '76 dream of launching themselves into the void, abdominal muscles clenched, bare-skinned.

Oh, the great adventure

Nadia does the rounds of the post-Olympic Western homages accompanied by Dorina, the marvellous casting of a queen and her more ordinary follower. Alongside them on the television sets is an interpreter who is a 'Romanian federal monitor', someone to watch their words for them.

The 'interpreter's' tension is obvious – it's a live transmission – when the presenter wants to know whether the girls are in a hurry to get back to Romania after the month they have spent in Montreal. Her relief when they are enthusiastic about the idea of leaving the West. The interview is almost over, a lengthy advertisement for the benefits of a communist childhood.

The ever-smiling presenter enquires, 'What will you do when all this is over?' The child is hunched in a huge leather armchair, her legs slightly apart as she has fun swinging it from right to left. 'I don't think about it,' she replies, like someone covering their ears. 'Of course not, darling, but… tell us, when all this is finished, Nadia, do you intend to get married?' The question has only just been uttered when Nadia blows out her cheeks and withdraws still farther into the twisting armchair; her synthetic yellow roll-neck creases over her concave abdomen, she tightens the elastic on her left bunch.

And now, a topic that is hard to bring up, but is inevitable. The presenter with her bulky chignon lowers her voice and leans towards the monitor, stuffed into her blue suit. She nods her agreement, yes, it's true, it's inevitable.

'How can I put it... look, sweetheart, Olga now... she has... grown. What will you do?... When you start to lose?'

The child stares at the two women for a long moment. Then with a faintly mischievous smile, she pulls herself out of the abyss: 'I never think of losing. This is only a start.' Mollified, they allow a child to be a child and to finish the interview ask her to sing something in Romanian, a folk song perhaps? The little girl wrinkles her nose, turns to her companion, they put their heads together and whisper conspiratorially, then Nadia sits bolt upright in her chair and, like a declaration of independence, a diagonal without any red bows in her hair, she offers her pallid, bare cheeks to the TV lights and starts to sing, looking straight into the cameras, a French nursery rhyme. '*Je suis un petit garçon de bonne figure / Je suis un petit garçon oh, la belle aventure.*'

That summer of 1976, the numbers continue to mount up around Nadia: five thousand calls received by the Canadian Gymnastic Federation in less than three months, in the United States sixty per cent more calls to the emergency services: the girls who wanted to 'play at Nadia' have broken wrists or ankles.

It's as if they are no longer afraid of anything, they're real tomboys, complain the parents of young girls in the West who dangle from the highest branches of trees and have supper in their leotards, sweaty and with wild hair. It's a phase. They'll get over it.

Snapshots

26–27 July 1976

The front page of an American daily carries the headline 'BYE-BYE NADIA', she is shown facing a microphone held by a man's hand, she is clutching a brown doll with a drooping head.

– At Montreal airport, hundreds of people recognize her and want to touch her bunches, and she is crushed against the Air Canada counter. Nadia is eventually led to the safety of an office, where the hostess bends down to her and strokes her cheek – 'so cute' – while offering her a glass of water, and a pilot tells the journalists that, yes, he remembers a year or two earlier when he was flying from Bucharest to London and she was on board with her team and was allowed to come into the cockpit. She asked him loads of questions about the flight. Then a day or two ago he came across her on the television, and the judges gave her 10! 'I was so proud... my little girl...!'

At Bucharest airport, seven thousand people are waiting for her. When they all rush onto the tarmac, the aeroplane is forced to come to a halt a long way from its regular slot. This is nothing like the arrival of those foreign heads of state they are obliged to turn up for, lining the avenues, holding a flag and forcing a smile. Here, Party officials in military uniforms struggle to contain an entire city that is waving, throwing flowers, holding up multi-coloured placards, some men have climbed the lamp-posts and are clinging on, cameras at the ready.

Dressed in a lavender suit, the team's official dress, knee-length skirt, she puts a foot on the steps, carrying a bunch of red carnations an air hostess has given her, but then she pauses and retreats back inside the cabin, I can't, Professor, I want to stay here, she clings on to his sleeve, but he grows angry, he has promised the Central Committee photos, General Mladescu himself has taken the trouble to come to greet this little kid who now acts as if she has discovered a monster under her bed in the middle of the night. Through the aircraft's open door, they can hear the joyous 'NA-DI-A, NA-DI-A' from the expectant crowd. Without a word, Dorina straightens Nadia's ponytail, gently pushes her towards the exit. Béla tries to make his way forward, but the crowd is too dense, a microphone appears and dances awkwardly in front of Nadia's mouth, as she says, 'I have brought back three gold medals, which I dedicate to the Party, to my home country and to the Romanian people.' But this is barely audible, because a chorus of children is shouting 'BRA-VO NA-D-I I I-A!'. A journalist grabs her by the arm, Do it again, he says, again, Béla pushes him away, Nadia rubs her arm, Béla strokes her soaking forehead, clasps her damp little hand, whispers in her ear, 'Start again, sweetie. Go on, sweetheart.'

The following day, *Scînteia* reproduces the telegram sent from Montreal to Nicolae and Elena Ceaușescu, thanking them for having given permission for this great victory and signed in hierarchical order: Nadia Dorina Mariana Anca Gabriela Luminița Iuliana.

– More than sixty thousand letters arrive in Onești from all over the world. Some of them are simply addressed to:

Miss Nadia Comăneci
Gymnast
Romania

– Two hundred thousand postcards with her picture on them are printed by the Romanian Post Office: they show her in the final pose of her floor exercise. In a white leotard, of course, her right foot pointed forward. And with a smile, the one which she now has to prove exists in order to silence her critics.

– There is only one thing they want, one wish: to see the little girl. King Hussein of Jordan, Jimmy Carter, Giscard d'Estaing, all of them dream of seeing her training during their official visits to Bucharest. What does she have to do to satisfy them? The Montreal performance, and especially that final pose, you know?

They are seated high up in the beautiful gym, she puffs out her cheeks as she steadies just in time after her tumbling diagonal. She stays up late, sitting at table with them in this fashionable restaurant reserved for influential people, diplomats and Securitate members, there are no children in Capşa, the waiters, starched white napkins folded over their forearms, bow to her ceremoniously, there is so much to eat, different kinds of meat, a variety of sauces, she is even allowed a sip of wine.

She poses between two generals. She poses in the living room of her home, seated on the old duck-egg-blue sofa that's been recovered in a golden yellow fabric, with her father wearing a suit for the occasion, gazing at her, turned towards her as she pretends to be sorting stamps in the album on her knees. The photographer has asked her to wear yellow socks to go with her red jacket and blue tracksuit trousers.

In her school uniform with a white hairband, blouse buttoned up to the neck under her navy-blue smock, she poses, serious-looking, surrounded by her classmates, a blurry mass of hands held out ecstatically towards the medals she is wearing round her neck.

She poses with Béla in the gymnasium garden, with orchid-bows decorating her bunches. They appear to be discussing work, she is the collaborator in miniature of the world architecture they have built.

She poses in her bedroom, surrounded by her dolls 'from the five continents' carefully arranged on the bed by her mother.

She poses in a traditional Romanian blouse.

She poses on the beach in a citrus yellow two-piece, holding a red ball aloft. Nadia's well-earned vacation! She poses surrounded by children in bathing costumes for whom she is signing autographs.

With the other girls in the team, on the sand, in her track-suit (during this week of holidays offered them by the Party, they train each morning from 7 to 9, do balancing exercises on the beach, then it's lunch, an obligatory siesta, and when they wake up an hour's swimming followed by a race on the seashore to strengthen their ankles, before a 'relaxed' training session prior to supper).

She poses in the snow, the other little girls in single file behind her are wearing skis, but Nadia has to take them off after the photo because Béla won't allow her to risk a fall.

She poses surrounded by adults in military uniforms (the paunchy general clings on to her hand for the photo, Nadia can hear his heavy breathing, his hand is podgy and soft).

On a stage, opposite an immense portrait of herself on the façade of a building, a little girl with harsh, haughty features.

This book of photographs devoted to her ends with an image of the ceremony in the Congress Palace, at which she is conse-crated a Heroine of Socialist Labour, there has never been anyone so young, because normally this title is reserved for mothers with many children. She is the New Child of progress, even more modern than the Romanian oil industry, which is expanding rapidly.

In profile, she smiles at Ceauşescu. Still dressed in the team's lavender suit, she leans forward into the microphone and recites in a high-pitched voice, 'I am very touched. From the hand of the most beloved person in Romania! I will never forget this August day. Nor your belief in my strength, nor that of our esteemed Comrade Elena. We, all the girls in the team, have felt the warmth of your paternal love and we thank you from the bottom of our souls, beloved Conducător.' He raises a hand and the applause dies away. 'Here is a young girl born in a socialist country and rewarded with the highest accolades in world sport!' Each of the Great Leader's phrases is punctuated by 'sustained' applause, as the official communiqué describes it.

She poses with Béla, who bends down to be on the same level as her for the camera lens. He himself is awarded the Order of Labour First Class, a medal given to men and women who teach excellence to young Romanians. Every morning at the start of their training session, he greets the girl who has received a more prestigious honour than he has with the words, 'Ah! Here comes our sacred, decorated cow!'

From Romania with love, Nadia

1977

'That must have been quite something, the arrival of the CBS Entertainment team in Onești...'

'Oh yes! People crowded round Flip and the technicians' truck. No one had ever seen a black man in Onești before.'

'And how did Flip Wilson take it?'

(She laughs.)

'He drank tsuica plum brandy with everybody from first thing in the morning, so they had to wait for him to sober up before they could start filming!'

'He was the one who introduced Béla to the American public and made him a character in the tale the media spun around you...'

'The Americans adored Béla from the start. He did everything to please them...'

'Such as?'

'Oh, you know, those phrases he'd learned before they shot the film, "Winning is everything", or "Show me a good loser and I'll show you a loser". That sort of stuff.'

'Don't those incredible opening credits remind you of something?'

'No... a film?'

'...The Six Million Dollar Man, with you in the role of Steve Austin!'

'The reason for my trip is a young girl. I fell in love with her at the same time as you did, millions of TV viewers.' It is with these words from Flip Wilson, presenter and comic superstar, that the American prime-time show begins: *From Rumania with Love, Nadia*. A brisk soundtrack underscores the opening credits, a series of smiling faces: first the supporting roles: Dorina, Luminiţa, Mariana, Márta, in multicoloured split screens, then Béla himself, given a close-up of several seconds, and finally, to a roll of drums and brass, we zoom in on the face of a laughing Nadia.

Opening sequence: Flip Wilson pants as he tries to keep up with Nadia, making despairing gestures to camera as she runs way ahead of him; they are both wearing Romanian team track-suits. Cross-fade to the two of them in the gym, Flip is standing on the beam, she holds his hand as he cries out, 'Mom, I'm scared!' Then Flip Wilson surrounded by golden-skinned children dressed in heavy white shirts embroidered with red, blue and green flowers; they applaud the presenter politely before joining hands in a traditional round, accompanied by a group of wrinkled old musicians bussed in from Bucharest, professionals, the young musicians in Oneşti are only interested in the Stones and don't know how to play any of the folk songs the Americans want to hear.

Flip Wilson, his back to a shiny red sun, holds a bunch of golden grapes up to the camera, says, 'These grapes' – he bites one, closes his eyes, 'mmmm – they're unforgettable, my friends, and this bread' – a woman in a flowery headscarf hands him a thick slice – 'this bread, wow! has made me forget what we call bread in our country, bah!' With that, he throws a loaf of soft white bread wrapped in plastic over his shoulder. The final shot pulls back to show the children clustered in the middle of a meadow singing a nostalgic song, Flip hugs Nadia while he says to camera, 'I'll be there in the stands at Moscow, and I'll blow kisses to my Nadia!'

Even more than Nadia, what this programme promotes is Romania. A joyful Romania. And here it is not the decimal point that is misplaced, it's a word that has been disappeared: communist. Although it is never pronounced, this is what is in fact being praised throughout this unbelievable American promo for an innocent, spring-like communism with young pioneers bursting with health. A tacit co-production between Romania and the United States, because the programme contains no interview with Nadia, and when she talks to Béla, their conversations are not translated.

Then, enchanted by the frail little communist's white leotard, girls in the West trample on cold wars. Hungry to be tested and judged ruthlessly, for being woken at dawn, for air without air-conditioning, for national anthems and hard work, consumed by the desire to be part of it, consumed by their self-sacrifice, armies of small Simone Weils answer the call and leave for gym camps in Romania, challenging the saccharine world that awaits them on their return.

Comrade

Such is the man. Such is the political leader. Such is Ceauşescu, the president who accepts no honour other than that of leading his people, like Moses, to the promised land of prosperity and independence.

M.-P. HAMELET,
Le Figaro journalist, 1971

How to describe him. He is incredible statistics, exponential graphs, constantly increasing production of wheat and vegetables, spectacular growth for the country. He is the vigour, the director, the driver, the beacon. He doesn't take sides between China and the USSR, participates in the preparations for the Helsinki Accords, talks even-handedly to West and East Germany, receives Arafat without breaking with Israel after the Six-Day War. On 15 August 1968 he leaves for Prague to offer his support to Dubček, and on his return declares to a huge crowd in Bucharest, 'Romania condemns the invasion of Russian tanks in Czechoslovakia!' Romania. Condemns. These two words never before placed alongside each other are applauded as far away as the United States. In France, General de Gaulle congratulates himself on this 'healthy breeze blowing in the east' and awards him the Grand Cross of the Legion of Honour. Delighted with the reception he receives in Bucharest, Nixon emphasizes the obvious similarities between the United States and Romania.

There were the Eastern and the Western blocs. He slips between the two, finds a way between one and the other.

What to call him? Comrade seems too familiar for someone who, the moment he was appointed president, ordered an architect to design a regal sceptre for the inauguration. General Secretary of the Communist Party, President of the State Council, President of the Socialist Republic and Supreme Helmsman, all rolled into one. He is the engineer of the future, he constructs the narrative in which they are all to live. He holds out his hand to you: take your place in the story, become part of whatever I imagine. The Comrade talks without even taking time to pause for breath. He declaims, proclaims. The Comrade takes all the parts, and the public applauds. He is resistance against the Russians! He is redis-covered national pride! The man who can dialogue with Western heads of state! Their modern partner, an Eastern Kennedy who nonetheless does not disregard traditions, a monarch from the Middle Ages surrounded by his knights dressed in medieval garb for the national feast day. He is celebrated, feted by poets and writers who sing his praises as 'the planet's pre-eminent thinker', 'the one who has breathed life back into life', 'the thinking pole star, the Danube of thought'. And everyone participates in the building of this new enterprise that is Romania, everybody has a role to play, a message to hold aloft in the stadiums, long live our beloved Conducător!

The country is a rough, shapeless cloth in urgent need of restoration, a filthy peasant's rag. A cloth that ends up adopting whatever shape it is given, but which loses its shape so quickly it has to be repaired constantly... the rhythm accelerates, we have to make sure that the narrative is the one the Comrade has created, without any errors: legions of revisers and correctors read the articles printed in *Scînteia*, the national daily, to make sure his name, cited more than thirty times on each page, is spelled properly. CEAUŞESCU.

It is not only words that are needed, but images as well: children. Dressed in white, holding their hands out to him, radiant. And towards her, Comrade Elena, that triumph of will and progress, a woman of humble physique and origins who has become 'the greatest scientist of international renown', covered in diplomas thanks to her thesis on polymers, obtained in secret at a university barred to students and guarded by police. Elena, 'honourable engineer, doctor, head of the National Council of Science and Technology', the New Woman, mother and at the same time minister of Science, Education, Justice and Health, Elena, around whom flutter the doves released before the filming of the countless reports devoted to her. And the lustrous Nadia is the sign of their success, the New Child they applaud because now she is the spectacle.

'You've done your research,' she says after a prolonged silence... 'I'm not saying that what you've written did not exist, but you've analysed it a posteriori. *It was very different to how you describe it. This will shock you, because I know the certainties your supposed liberal democracies have about these things... but there was also a kind of... joy in the 1970s, even though that doesn't change anything, obviously. I detest the films and novels that talk about eastern Europe, all those clichés. Grey streets. Grey people. The cold. When I tell Westerners that in Bucharest in summer the heat is stifling, they look at me as if I were off my head, even nowadays! Let's try not to make my life or those years into a bad, simplistic movie. Goodnight to you.'*

She hangs up so speedily I don't get the chance to tell her about my meeting with Mihaela G., a sociologist who explains to me why gymnastics so quickly became a priority sport for those in power in

Romania: the gymnasts didn't eat very much, they were very profitable; too young to have an opinion about what was going on in their country, they were not going to ask for asylum whenever they had a meet in the West.

The little girl from Oneşti brings glory to Romania from the tips of her gym shoes, she makes communism sparkle in the picture-postcard image of a pure white leotard with a red star, the purity of her appetite for hard work is venerated in a West desperate for a secular angel.

The Russians fascinated the whole world with their Sputnik, and they and the United States are bound to keep their military superiority. For its part, Romania makes of the ones Béla likes to call his 'little girl missiles' the most adorably fascinating show on earth thanks to his supreme weapon: the bomb Nadia C., who performs what American specialists describe as 'pure madness, a biomechanical impossibility'. Until, that is, the chief choreographer himself becomes irritated at this tiny shadow who puts him in the shade: Ceauşescu, Mihaela tells me, gives an order in 1981 for singing, dancing and gymnastics competitions to be held throughout Romania in order to obliterate the image of the heroic youngster he himself crowned.

Like a dog

E arly in spring 1977, she is carefully got ready. Her mother has ironed the lavender suit she hasn't worn since the previous summer, the waist button has had to be moved because it was too tight, they do her hair, hesitating between a ponytail and bunches, even though she's not going to a competition.

Just before leaving the house, Márta, who is accompanying her to Bucharest, inspects her and suggests Stefania puts some rouge on her cheeks, the kid looks a fright. Her mother refuses, 'No, that's enough as it is,' then stops short, as if caught out. What if Márta and Béla, who are close to you-know-who, reported to the high-ups that what she really said was, 'That is quite enough already'? They might think she and her husband are hostile to the regime, are sceptical about the national celebrations surrounding their daughter, that national symbol. Possibly even planning to escape abroad, we must keep our eye on them, I'm relying on you, Márta. The parents of a heroine like our Nadia have to be above reproach, if they prove unsuitable, we'll find some others.

Nadia has already met the Comrade: he rose slowly out of his seat (a throne) and came to shake her hand at the ceremony in her honour.

'But this is special,' she is told, 'you must be so proud, he's going to receive you personally, like a government minister!'

Do all the ministers have to wash their hands? she asks the lady who, the moment she arrives, leads her to a bathroom with such smooth white walls they seem to be a reproach to everything that isn't equally smooth and white. She hesitates for a moment before turning the tap, it's a swan's neck, should she grasp it by the beak or take it by the neck to switch off the hot water? And when they reach his office, everything goes wrong. The Most Renowned Scientist in the World is there, and snaps at Nadia when she immediately sits down, 'Stand up, are you already tired?' Did she choose the wrong chair? It's so hard to know, she has never been in a room with so many possibilities, all these embroidered, upholstered seats, some of them in red velvet, others eau de Nil, sofas and carpets softer than the ones in the gym.

He has his back to her. The sunlight gently striping the dark room glints on his brilliantined black and grey hair, nobody says a word, and she is thirsty. The Comrade is standing erect, and his dark grey suit seems to be obeying his every gesture. Like an Orthodox priest, but priests smell of old wood and dampness. He is more like a father, not a papa, a father, more decent than a family.

Afterwards, she is asked a thousand times what it was like, and she makes it up a little because she doesn't want to mention the episode with the chair, or that the Most Renowned Scientist in the World said about her to the Conducător as though she was not in the room, 'She's put on a hell of a lot of weight, hasn't she?' before hustling her out, 'Go on, go on,' as quickly as possible.

American intermezzo: the trial

September 1977

The television programme she is sent to New York for isn't a trial – not a real one, anyway. The programme so many people saw, all those people in their dining rooms having supper – my goodness, the fairy has put on weight – is so hurtful, humiliating, as if someone were pulling her trousers down and forcing her to confess out loud, 'Yes, I've got my period.' Because that's what it's about, isn't it? They talk about her in sad, disbelieving voices, they repeat, 'My, but you have... changed,' which means 'you have periods now', and there she is, a fat fucking pudding who can't get up from her chair and leave but instead sinks farther and farther into it with the presenter's every new question.

She dreams she cries out, or perhaps she really does cry out, yet it can't be real because if she did her mother would come running, of course, and here nobody comes when she bursts into tears after the programme. Sitting in the make-up room where they are wiping off the too-dark foundation she lowers her eyes to her thighs, which are thicker even than the day before, her mother won't come, she's so far off, and anyway who, tell me who, could restrain this flesh growing like a bulimic flower, arrogant and brutal, demanding the right to take her over bit by bit.

The trial is to be televised and takes place in three minutes thirty-nine seconds as part of an American entertainment programme. No need for a lawyer. The accused, Nadia C., is accompanied by a Romanian woman introduced as her interpreter. During the trial, we learn that the 'interpreter' isn't on the side of the accused, but is instead the strange lawyer representing a group comprising the coach Béla Károlyi and the Romanian Gymnastic Federation, as well as the huge number of TV viewers who feel cheated, deceived by this new appearance of the aforementioned Nadia C. (all those letters received after the broadcast of the European Championships, complaining they no longer recognize their Montreal elf).

Irrefutable facts are presented, tape measure and weighing machine in hand, scientific evidence. The prosecution is careful to maintain a courteous tone when it addresses the child hunched in her chair in her red roll-neck sweater.

Presenter: 'Since Montreal we've heard that you've put on a few kilos... have you been ill?'

The interpreter, in Romanian, to Nadia, 'Compared to Montreal, you are fatter and your work is much worse.' The sound engineer signals to the presenter that, despite the HF mike, the girl's reply is inaudible, an embarrassed half-murmur.

Presenter: 'And yet there's one thing that hasn't changed, Nadia, you still speak very softly, are you just as shy?'

The interpreter, annoyed: 'He's asking you to speak up.'

A smile, a breath, almost an excuse.

Presenter: 'One day, Nadia, you'll have a daughter, would you like her to be a champion like you?'

Abruptly she cuts across the interpreter as she is about to 'translate': 'No, I haven't given it any thought, I have time, I have time.'

Managers in the West

B ack in 1977, a media triumvirate of three young girls reigned in the West. Jodie Foster plays a child prostitute in *Taxi Driver*, roaming the sidewalks of New York in high heels and mini-shorts. 'Are you really twelve and a half?' worries the character played by Robert de Niro. 'Hey, Jodie, have you got a boyfriend, when are you going to get married?' asks the journalist interviewing the actress on his programme.

Brooke Shields, too, plays a prostituted child in Louis Malle's *Pretty Baby*, a virgin in a cream guipure dress, sold at auction in a turn-of-the-century brothel.

'I want you to be my lover,' she whispers to Keith Carradine while the soundtrack plays a nostalgic Scot Joplin tune. 'Mmmm, you have quite a come-on look… Do you know what that expression means?' a mocking talk-show host asks Brooke Shields. Embarrassed, the little girl murmurs, 'Not really, no.' Then the presenter flicks through a magazine and holds it up to the camera, 'Mmm, so much the better. Tell me, do you think you're sexy in this photo?'

Aged ten, she posed naked in a bath, her smooth, slender body covered in oil, her face thick with make-up. Silent, Brooke rubs her nose and turns to the photographer sitting on the set beside her. He says enthusiastically, 'What a vamp! That photo is of a naked young girl who looks like a little boy who wants to look like a woman.' He's in the pay of Playboy Press, contributing the photograph to a publication devoted to very young girls: *Sugar and Spice*.

Nadia C. is the third young girl. For the girls in the West, the communist child with her make-up-free face gives them a taste of what war is all about. The best line of attack is to launch their straining bodies as hard as they can.

'I went to New York in 1977 for a competition. On Broadway there were these huge billboards showing a young girl the same age as me, advertising a perfume, I think. I was fascinated. I wasn't that kind of... I wasn't a girl who dreamed of becoming a woman. I wasn't a boy either. I kept myself... somewhere else. Outside all that.'

Lacquered chestnut brown bunches frame her blue gaze and long mascaraed eyelashes, her glossy lips half open as she clutches a beige teddy bear to her; the little girl in a white dress Nadia remembers so well is eight years old when she becomes the face of Love's Baby Soft perfumes. At the bottom of the poster, the slogan 'Because innocence is sexier than you imagine...'

Prague 1977:
European Championships

They are packed up against the security barrier, where is she, she hasn't come, then one of them shouts: 'Nadia!' He points her out to the others, and they all crowd round the Romanian team, calling out her name, is it really her, she has a new haircut! They raise their cameras, snap off photos blindly as if she has been in an accident and they want to capture every last detail of the damage, desperate to get the best angle for the communist badge on her leotard, creased by the wide elastic strap of the brassiere digging into her breasts.

Béla, the man who has calculated everything, who has invented the super-childhood of the young machine-like girls – I just *know*, he used to tell Western journalists asking how he could spot them so young – now Béla feels tired, almost defeated. 'What did you think, that she would never grow up?' Geza asks sarcastically, to which Béla replies with the self-confidence of a scientist: 'No, obviously I'm aware all this is perfectly normal. But… people are no longer accustomed to these… women's bodies.'

The whole world is no longer accustomed to them. And it is Béla and Márta, those geometricians of the air, who have put an end to the imprecise grace of the predecessors. They have given birth to a voracious baby. Gymnastics federations all over the world have changed their points systems, ever since the Comăneci salto it is danger that counts, accidents avoided by a hair's breadth, the inconceivable has to be produced.

Where have they come from, these girls, conceived in barely a year? Younger, leaner, smaller, meteors with no rear-view mirrors who have scarcely even heard of Ludmilla and her old-fashioned grace. Maria Filatova is fifteen, is one metre thirty-three centimetres tall and weighs thirty kilos, there are enormous bows round her bunches as if to help disguise her over-developed quads. On the beam, her arrogant chin seems to be pulled by the end of a steel cable somebody is drawing out from inside her miniaturized being. Number 8, another Soviet gymnast, is only there as a substitute, but Elena Moukhina stands on the top bar before launching into an unheard-of somersault between the two bars. A lot of girls like her, inspired by Nadia, need to be found and produced, because whereas before you could adjust for some imprecision in a shoulder movement, now the speed with which the exercises are performed means that is no longer possible. It's make or break.

In an email to Nadia I mention the punctuation in the articles written about her comeback a year after Montreal, exclamation marks that compete with the ellipses: '50kg!!!' 'Nadia is now a real woman ... ...' she confirms, 'It's true, it shouldn't be called female gymnastics, the spectators don't come to see women... You know, if competition leotards are always long-sleeved, it's to hide the girls' arms. Our biceps, our veins. Because above all we mustn't look too masculine either!'

Under our protection

The first version I write about the incident during the European Championships in Prague is in a farcical vein. A president who orders them to leave an international competition because he feels his team has been unfairly marked down makes Ceaușescu seem more Ubuesque than real. Nadia has read these pages, and they seem to amuse her. But as we are about to hang up, she adds, 'That day... it's only a small detail, but the Securitate guy picked me up under his arm like a... suitcase. Without a word.'

The chapter as I have rewritten it is not then the story of a dictator, but of this body-suitcase that judges, president and several coaches fight over and claim, with the excuse of protecting her. A new episode in this silent film, their all-consuming passion for a young girl who never gets asked what she thinks. What she has been offering for years now perhaps goes beyond words. She certainly defies translation.

On this very soft autumn Sunday, his guests drowsy after an excellent lunch, like thousands of Romanians the Comrade is sitting in front of his television watching the live broadcast of the Championships. Béla Károlyi appears on the screen, but no one in the room makes any comment about the Hungarian of 'cohabitant' nationality (recently it is deemed wise to avoid the term 'minorities', which angers the Comrade. 'We're all Romanians here, descendants of the Dacians, no divisions in our country!')

Besides, Béla brings back medals and lots of foreign currency, the Americans, Japanese and French can't get enough of their gym exhibitions.

Nadia has just beaten the Soviet girl with Chinese eyes, Nellie Kim, 'she doesn't even have a Slav name, that Chink!' She readjusts her leotard round her buttocks and walks towards the podium to receive her gold medal. One moment. What's going on? The TV camera zooms in on the Soviets, who are carrying Nellie Kim on high as she blows kisses to the stands. 'It's hard to understand what is... the Soviets have... have they won this event? No, it's not... did they win?' stammers the Romanian commentator. The Comrade hauls himself off the sofa, apoplectic, his voice hoarse with emotion. 'Romania condemns this... aggression! The judges are in the pay of the Russians and their bastard!' Now he is standing, on the point of vomiting, the others are turned towards him, waiting for him to restore order to things, children, everyone endlessly hoping he will congratulate, condemn, show them the way.

Booing from the TV set, the public are on their feet, just as angry, the camera tracks from the Soviets to Nadia in profile, hands on hips, the Soviet girls look tiny next to her.

He must make a decision worthy of this historic instant, this stutter in history, the Russians, Czechoslovakia. 'Get the aircraft ready at once!'

'The aircraft, Comrade? Are you... leaving for Prague?'

'No, you imbecile. Bring them back here! Interrupt the competition!'

Contact is immediately made with the ambassador. 'It's Sunday, my assistants are away,' he insists, before realizing he is being told to go to the stadium himself. His mission: to put an end to the humiliation, a real declaration of war.

Béla might well boast that nothing the Soviets do surprises him, may they vanish up their mother's cunt, but now a line has been crossed. His little calf may still be on the fat side, but he'll train her until she's back in human shape, and she has just crushed Nellie on the vault, but now the voice over the loudspeakers is blaring out that there has been a miscalculation: the gold medal is to go to Nellie, and the silver to Nadia! Béla roars at the public, 'Did you see that? Did you see the results dance to the dirty Russian tricks? The scores are changing all on their own on the board!' Impassive, Nadia is already walking towards the next event. And she scores a 10 on the uneven bars! Béla is exultant, that girl is a fucking scorpion, the girls on the team raise their fists to their queen, their faces beaming with a fierce delight. They all acclaim her. 'Na-di-a Na-di-a!' She runs over to Béla, who hugs her to him, her brutal little heart against his chest, he knows she is no longer thinking of the gold medal that's just been stolen from her, but about what comes next, as always. One last event, just one, and she can still win the title. It's her turn in a few seconds, Na-di-a Na-di-a, the judges call her name. She moves towards the beam and closes her eyes, takes a deep breath in the silence torn by flashbulbs.

The ambassador has finally succeeded in persuading the security guards to let him approach Béla. Stupefied by the dull faces of the girls hollow-eyed from exhaustion, by how skinny their thighs are, the violence with which their hips smash against the bars, the ambassador barely has time to explain why he is there. 'Comrade Károlyi, I am the Romanian ambassador, the Comrade's aircraft is waiting for you,' before this animal of a Hungarian tells him to go to the devil, him, his aeroplane and the supreme Comrade as well, with all Romania in it for good measure. The Hungarian has gone as close as possible to the mat; panting, hands together, he mutters to Nadia, 'Yes, that's right, sweetheart, go on, yes, gently, straighten up and you, ge… ently, that's right…' as though he was guiding her across the void. Ten! The crowd erupts, adoring, and Béla shouts hoarsely to the Comrade's henchmen who are grabbing him: 10, 10, 10!

She is allowed three minutes' rest before the next event. Nadia drops into a chair, her back soaked with sweat, drinks a few mouthfuls of water, Béla is some way off, apparently arguing with a group of officials. The other girls in the team are putting on their tracksuit bottoms, even though it is hot in the gym. Nadia conscientiously stretches her legs, the quivering hamstrings. Then he is alongside her. Seizes her arm, this stranger in a grey suit, he is so close with his sour breath, she stiffens, stammers, 'Coach, Coach!' at Béla, who is also surrounded by grey suits, then louder, Co-oach, she struggles, Béla strains towards her, bracing himself, but there are too many of them holding him back, I'm here, baby, we'll sort this out. Nadia can't hear him in the huge storm of the crowd whistling and booing, the scrum of photographers tries to catch one final shot of the Romanian girls, they walk slowly in a row without looking back, escorted all the way, towards the exit.

And on this autumn Sunday, commentators from every country repeat with consternation, 'This has never been seen before. Never. The Romanian girls are leaving the competition. Unfortunately, in her absence, Nadia's gold medal will go automatically to Nellie Kim.'

They are ushered onto the bus, then crammed onto the private plane. It's because war is brewing, Dorina says with a shudder; some of the girls are crying in their seats, the others are playing cards. No hostesses, only the usual interpreter, who is extremely nervous. Béla sits next to Nadia. In front and behind them, grey suits. He puts his hand on her warm one, squeezes it gently, a strange pain shackling his tongue; Nadia's small fingers grip his firmly, calm now, trusting him. The pilot announces: Three thousand. No, five thousand. I'm told there are ten thousand people waiting for us at the airport! The sports minister has insisted live on the radio: We will never allow ourselves to be humiliated by the Soviets! Our Comrade has brought back the tearful little girl. To put an end to her calvary, to protect our national baby, the heroic Nadia! The plane comes to a stop, the crowd rushes towards it, frantic, enraged, distraught, Where is she, we want to give her shelter, save her from all harm, keep her warm, under our protection.

Decree 770: dead or alive

'We were the land of children,' Madalina L. explains – she is a Romanian university lecturer whom I meet in Paris – before stressing that she isn't talking about communist pioneers in their white gloves, those mini-soldiers and their forced enthusiasm, but the way people spontaneously kissed chubby-cheeked youngsters on buses.

'People took them on their knee without even knowing them, showered them with presents even if they had nothing themselves. Kids were supported and encouraged to such an extent that some of them simply had to become champions at something, like Radu Postăvara, the five-year-old orchestra conductor who went on international tours. It was a drama if you weren't outstanding. And I imagine you know it was a crime not to produce children.

'Decree 770... it was... a war against women... in 1966, Ceauşescu outlawed abortion, he wanted new generations who would be raised under his exclusive ideology. It worked for a few years, the many babies born then were known as the decreteii. Around 1973, the growth rate began to stagnate, because women started to organize as best they could, even if from 1975 on it became almost impossible to get a passport. Then Ceauşescu took it into his head to pay off all the country's foreign debts, and you know what happened: food was rationed, there was nothing to feed the children, nothing to feed them. Impossible. We... were afraid they would die of hunger, you understand? So then... some women *were lucky enough to meet Bulgarian or Polish women on holiday, they knew and offered their pills in secret; women took them any way they could, they didn't understand the instructions, they... I can't tell you, I'm sorry. If they became pregnant, it was... they performed their own... the... foetus... with their hand... so many died... bled to death in their kitchens, I...'*

Madalina falls silent for a long while. I suggest we continue some other day. 'It wouldn't be any different,' she murmurs.

'How can I describe it?' she goes on. 'I call it a "war" because... they were men, those doctors paid to supervise women's uteruses. And factory foremen were rewarded if a large number of their female workers fell pregnant. Agents in the hospitals were ordered to read women's files to discover those who were a few weeks pregnant, in order to stop them aborting.

'Do you know what I can't forgive you in the West for? In 1974, the UN proposed that Romania chair the World Population Conference, arguing that we had been able "to resolve the demographic crisis"! And Nadia, even without meaning to, was part of it, the incessant publicity for the Model Child. And the irony is that, as soon as she grew, Nadia couldn't escape either. She was "inspected" like all the rest of us, by the "menstruation police", those doctors who examined us every month in our workplaces and urged us to have yet more babies.

'In 1984 or 1985, I can't remember which, a woman died after an abortion. The Securitate forced her family to organize the funeral outside the factory, her body was exhibited as an example. An example... they exhibited living women's bodies as well, like Nadia, with those postcards of her everywhere, and her triumphs; dead or alive, we could be used.'

Rewrite

On 4 March 1977 at 21.22 hours, the city is on its knees. The media do not film any of the ruins, almost nothing of the eviscerated Bucharest, no interview is carried out with the survivors who recall an icy night when 'the sky was blood-red', that night when an earthquake turns the capital into a mortuary. Silence closely surrounds the catastrophe, a profound silence in the midst of which Romanians have no other choice but to try to guess the seriousness of what has happened, or to imagine it. Dozens of reports show Ceaușescu leaning over grateful wounded in the hospitals. In reality, when he visits, he refuses to shake the survivors' hands, and demands that all his entourage be disinfected.

The destruction is an invitation to the Comrade to rewrite the city, and he takes advantage of the ruins to flatten entire neighbourhoods. The fact is that peasant Romania disgusts him: it's smelly and dirty. Now not just the villages themselves, but all trace of the countryside in Bucharest must disappear too. The whole country has to become a city with no blind spots. Several days after the disaster, with the groans of those buried under the rubble still to be heard, Ceaușescu orders rebuilding to start.

I mention to Nadia a series of photos that appeared in the Romanian press at the time: she is posing with Dorina, both of them are wearing navy-blue overalls and are smiling at the camera, spades in hand.

'*Did you help with the rescue work?*'

'*...No, I wasn't in Romania, there was a meet abroad. I came back a few days later.*'

'*So those photos were a complete manipulation? The Model Child helping reconstruct her country...*'

(She interrupts me.)

'*It's what they call "marketing" nowadays, isn't it? As soon as I got back, I visited hospitals. Do you know something? We're never going to get anywhere if you don't understand a couple of things. All sportsmen and women who win are political symbols. They promote systems. Communism back in those days, capitalism now. And in your country...*'

(Her brief laugh at the far end of the line sounds ironic.)

'*You know that even in those days the brands sponsoring your female athletes stipulated in their contracts that they had to wear make-up, to wear dresses in preference to tracksuits when they appeared in public... do you think that's better, more... modern?*'

On her own

When Nadia became the junior champion in Romania, Stefania was very proud of her daughter: the title had something admirable and healthy about it. In the years that followed, Stefania let Comrade Károlyi deal with everything, she had no head for somersaults, no matter how clever. Because she was always thinking of the next morning, when from four o'clock she had to be one of the first to join the queue for the oil that had just been delivered to the grocer's; because every evening she came back exhausted from having waited for hours in the scorching sun for the meat she brings home wrapped in rags – that will do to pay the doctor; because she had to finish three pairs of trousers for the next day.

But now. Europe. The world. Magazines, American TV programmes. A doll created in her image. The Congress Palace in Bucharest packed with Party dignitaries, giving her a standing ovation. And the black limousines that park with increasing frequency outside their house to come to take Nadia or to bring her back from Bucharest. Alarming, worrying black limousines that draw everyone's attention to their house. The neighbours are suspicious, and Stefania can understand why. Sometimes, when Nadia eats with them on Saturday nights, it seems to her she can spot a new sense of authority in her daughter's face, something that excludes the possibility of sharing any secrets or doubts. A child who opens the door to people in uniforms, to official cars, an honoured guest in front of whom she hesitates to speak, a child who stares at her, unsmiling.

'You mistrust your own daughter now!' Gheorghe shouted at dinner one evening when she signalled to him to be quiet, he was telling a joke about the Comrade that he had heard in the garage. You can't mistrust your own daughter, can you?

'What was Nadia Comăneci like as a baby?' a journalist asks Stefania the week before. He pronounces Co-ma-ne-ci as if she might not know her daughter's name. And it's 'Eeny-meeny-miny-mo' that she recalls, or 'this little piggy went to market…' We used to play in the garden, and I would hold her to me, all soft and out of breath from running, she always wanted to run and to do everything on her own – *singurica singura* – do her own hair, dress herself, she pushed away the spoonful of rice I offered her. And Gheorghe would tell the neighbours, Oh yes, she knows what she wants, of course it was easy for him to admire that, I also tried to admire her, but that wish in a three-year-old child constantly to separate herself from me, as though to prove how useless I was, sometimes made me feel like saying I don't know her, she isn't mine.

She wasn't with the rest of us, she would like to tell the journalist. She was on her own.

The Illness

Eeny-meeny-miny-what? Warily, Nadia lifts her T-shirt in front of the mirror. A desire to cry leaves her sitting on the rug in her bedroom, she takes a deep breath, waiting for this wave of sadness to pass. She doesn't want to. She doesn't want to any more. She is pierced through with misery. Her life, tough as a remote-controlled train, has come off the rails. Obedience is just one of the pieces missing from the perfect puzzle of her life up to now, with, among others: the constant hunger that makes it hard to sleep (to dream of eating, and to wake up at dawn terrified you almost did eat something), her hands scarred with blisters and tiny cuts that never heal, thighs tattooed with bruises ingrained in the veins, and muscles whose fibres are disintegrating, over-stretched tendons saved *in extremis* thanks to the indispensable codeine and cortisone.

She wishes she weren't there. Not to be forced to be there when the coach calls out the dimensions of her Illness in centi-metres and kilos. The best thing would be to catch a real illness, to be obliged to stay in bed and sleep beneath a blanket that would completely drown out the world outside. Sleep is now the only space where she can escape her sorrow for a few hours. This unacceptable betrayal, a sniggering uppercut: she would love to cut them off, these whatsits – she refuses to say the word breasts – this capitulation forcing her in the direction of all the others: the girls at high school. The ones Dorina now so wants to be like, whereas they had once agreed that these girls are soft, soft, soft, like the Romanian *rahat* sweet. They're so comfortable you can sink into them like cushions. And now, it makes her nauseous, she too has become comfortable. Ugly. Shapeless. She misses herself, oh yes, she misses herself, and also that tiny ritual Nadia used to perform in bed at night until the previous summer: to run her hand over her stomach, stretched between the two masts formed by her protruding hips, and then fall asleep, reassured.

The Illness is advancing. It's invading her, gnawing away at her previous existence. Its latest manifestation: last Friday as she sprints towards the vault. Everything seems normal. But as she runs, something else begins to move, a ridiculous, jolting movement: extra flesh that isn't part of her, but of which she can feel every quiver, every repugnant autonomous fatty cell. She pulls up short. Bursts into tears without getting up from the floor, where she has allowed herself to collapse from the shock of this fresh advance of her Illness; the others turn pale at the unspeakable outrage they are witnessing, in this gym where they never protest or complain.

And the organization, the time it takes now to try to continue to keep her Illness a secret: the thick protection weighing down her knickers, which she hides between the wall and the bookshelves where her dolls, her cups and her medals are displayed, piles of stained cloths and rags. She can't bring herself to cross the kitchen in front of her parents (sympathetic but disappointed, already missing their fairy) with 'that' in her hand and put it in the bin there, as though it was a normal part of her life, in among the potato peelings and yesterday's newspaper. She waits until late afternoon, hides the package wrapped in sheets of newspaper under her sweater, and gets rid of it like a worrying piece of evidence in the dustbin at the far end of the street. She has become a criminal with bloodstained fingers and graceless knickers.

They all seem to think it will pass, that it's not this leprosy invading her under their very eyes. They keep their distance, Béla, her father. At the end of the day, if he is satisfied, Béla lifts the little girls on his back and runs round the gym, they jump about laughing, their faces red with pleasure. I'll never again be able to sit astride someone's shoulders, Nadia tells herself as she watches them; perhaps he's worried something might ooze through her tights, she too is afraid that something might slip out of her without her being able to control it, she is split open, widened. Her sweat also seems to have grown denser; in the evening she sniffs her armpits, horrified to encounter the stubborn sourness typical of her mother's blouse. Ill. Undone from within. Béla slaps her awkwardly on the shoulders to encourage her, doubtless trying to find somewhere on her body that's not affected. You'll get over it, Márta promised her the day she found her in tears in the changing rooms. Everything is possible with today's medicines, sweetheart.

No. She was the invincible one, and that had nothing to do with the medals. They were all invincible, sharp and speedy, barely a year earlier, they stamped their feet into the ground as they ran, threw themselves into the dust, rolled in the grass, jumped in the river in their swimsuits, clung to their fathers, licked their fingers, the Moldovan summers allowed them to eat ice cream for dinner, they peered out over time itself. They could outrun everything.

Now time is shrinking. She is shrinking. Her thoughts are shrivelling, becoming those of an ill-spirited housewife, her ideas ever more hemmed-in, she has to take so many precautions not to be caught out. In the street she passes a young girl in a light-coloured pair of trousers and immediately thinks of the possibility of soiling the fabric. Her body has become a soft machine whose malfunctions she is terrified of. She would like simply to follow her own path, but that also has been modified by the Illness, is strewn with problems and fresh dangers. She hunches over so as not to attract the attention of men her father's age who stare at her mouth when she licks the ice cream cornet, the hungry look on the cleaner's face when she throws out her chest in the final salute, her father slightly withdrawing his pelvis when she throws herself into his arms; he kisses her on the forehead and gently pushes her away.

Her grandmother scolded her the previous Sunday when she was lying flat on her stomach in her nightdress to watch television, 'Sit up properly, aren't you ashamed of yourself?', at the same time glaring at Grandfather, slumped in his armchair behind her.

She has skipped training this afternoon, just as she did the day before yesterday, she's so tired. Where is my champion, sighed her mother, you're not going to stay in the bathroom crying your whole life, are you? Get over it and give me that to wash, you've sweated such a lot, do you think you've got an infection down there, sweetheart? You know that now you have to protect your leotard at all costs.

They tie their sweatshirts round their waists just in case, and get up warily, casting a discreet glance at the chair, not wanting to leave any trace. Brutally expelled from their realm, the former little girls float between East and West and fade away, while a note of apology and deodorized absence is left in their place. Sorry, they will no longer be able to take part.

The end

Two men have emerged from a black car with a Bucharest licence plate. They sit in the Comănecis' living room. The reason for their visit: to distance Nadia from the Hungarian – at her request, as she can no longer bear his methods – and from his stinking, backward countryside, and instead put her with a modern coach, with a Romanian name, in Bucharest. That way, Nadia will be more easily available for all the invitations, because everyone still wants to see the little girl. And they'll finally be able to take that peasant down a peg or two, the one who ever since Montreal has never stopped crowing, oblivious to any reprisals: 'If you don't like it, come and train these squirts yourselves.'

They sing the praises of the capital, the new, ultra-modern gym and the top-class high school. The boarding facilities are brand new, and of course she will always be able to come home during the school holidays. Her mother wipes her hands on a perfectly ironed cloth, apologizes for the shiny wooden floor she has just waxed, she's so tired, the damage Nadia is causing with all her rows, it might be a solution to put some distance between her and the coach. It's a trial, an amicable split, no one is angry, sweetheart. Her father shows the members of the Federation out, he's proud of this summit meeting, all because of his daughter and her future. It's too late that evening to tell Béla. She'll be leaving early the next morning. Nadia leaves her mother a note to take to

Dorina. 'I'm going to live in Bucharest!! You must come and see me!!! Your Nadia.'

The next morning, dawn splashes the gym as it fills with high-pitched voices greeting Béla one by one; they dip their hands in chalk before starting their daily warm-ups. Everything has already been wiped clean. Her name, NADIA COMĂNECI, on the locker. Her name, COMĂNECI NADIA, on the register. Torn from him very early this morning, his little girl, now painfully slightly less little.

They are preparing for the World Championships. The pianist takes his place. A new gymnast is warming up, her face is gaunt and her body so dry it doesn't even produce any sweat. Geza comes and sits next to him. They watch the new girl without a word. Geza asks gently, 'You know, don't you?' Béla nods. Then the two men fall silent, leaving a shred of an enchanting melancholy tune, 'That's my baby baby', a few notes from a pre-1929 Charleston and a fragrance they can't place drifting between the two of them.

When I reread my notes, this episode seems clear: Nadia rebels against Béla and his discipline, they argue all the time. For his part, Ceauşescu is looking for a chance to undermine Béla, who, although he is being watched and has his phone tapped, is no longer afraid of anything, not even the Securitate. The decision is made: she will train in Bucharest. Infuriated, Béla quits Oneşti and sets himself up in Deva, in the north of the country, where he opens a new school, a 'medals factory'.

I send Nadia this version. No, she replies, it's not right. She never really wanted to leave, it was the Romanian regime that took the decision without consulting her, they detested Béla.

A few days after this exchange, a Romanian magazine publishes an article contradicting her version and validating mine. The document is from the Securitate archives and reveals repeated messages Nadia sent at the time to the authorities, begging them to move her to Bucharest because she can't take any more. And when the Party refuses to separate them, fearing that without Béla she will start to lose, mention is made of Nadia's threats to commit suicide if she is not taken out of there.

At the far end of the line, at first she is quiet. Then she says drily:

'What more do you want to read? The gutter press? When are you going to trust me? Are the Securitate's secret files really your sources?'

'Anyone can look at the files now. Have you read the one on you?'

'No.'

'Will you, some day?'

'Never. Never. I have no wish to learn what I don't want to know, and besides, those who have done so have been destroyed by what they read.'

'Ah... what did they discover?'

'Well, almost everybody went to the authorities to tell them what they knew about their neighbours so that they would be left in peace. They didn't have much choice. But some people have discovered recently that their husband or their children were spying on them on behalf of the Securitate... So who are we to believe? Those files are full of lies from all those who wanted to get out of it as best they could.'

I hang up with the feeling that as we finish our conversation, she is trying to make me question all the versions I read, apart from her own.

Comrade Coach, the girls of the Dinamo Bucharest club call

him. He chews gum made in England, not the Romanian sort that disintegrates into little balls after only a few seconds; he uses a typewriter for his reports to the Securitate, which are always impeccable. 'We'll be working on the mental aspect, everything is in the mind,' he explains to them on the first day, with a smile. He acknowledges Béla's results and methods, 'solid, old-fashioned', in the way you might praise an ox pulling a rattling cart.

Everything in the gym is brand new, the showers are gleaming, and there is a dedicated masseuse for the girls. Nadia gets on well with Livia, the daughter of an important Party member, who is always accompanied by her follower, who laughs at her jokes at the right moment and applauds her friend on the beam. Like Dorina and you, Livia remarks.

Dorina, who writes to her twice a week. Every Thursday and Monday, Nadia receives letters that Dorina sprinkles with perfume (the evaporated alcohol takes the colour out of the paper and blots the ink, so these words are carefully rewritten). Dorina writes everything in capitals: DO YOU THINK OF US (me?). Dorina is also having to face the consequences of the Illness, writes down everything she eats in a notebook (I'm so dreadfully HUNGRY, you can't imagine), goes running in the woods at six in the morning with Márta, and has decided not to attempt anything new for the championships (If I can at least manage to stuff my fat ARSE into a leotard and do not bring shame on my country...).

Nadia's Illness, though, has eased somewhat. She hardly thinks about it. No time. In the evening, Livia takes her dancing in clubs where there are few Romanians, mostly Frenchmen and Americans. Nadia asks them to play 'In the Summertime' by Mungo Jerry and has just one cocktail, staying absurdly faithful to Béla.

Is your name Nadia, like the gymnast? they ask, unable to believe it. She is 'like the gymnast'. The previous week a boy (a man!) holds her tight, they are dancing, he thrusts his knee between her legs, his hot breath on her hair, she has no idea what kind of response she is supposed to make, he says, 'Don't play at being the baby, don't be difficult, you know you've got a great ass, did you fuck an American in Montreal? Shit, look at those bruises, has someone been beating you up?' Embarrassed, she covers her thighs as quickly as possible.

Eeny-meeny-miny-what? And what does he want her to do, pushing her head down like that? She sits back down in the car, slightly nauseous, her cheeks bright red, he lends her a handker-chief to wipe herself with. She focuses, tries hard not to see in these poses something she must do better, or refine. Her thighs wide open like a chicken about to be stuffed. It's so inelegant being unable to move like this, he's got hold of her knees, giving her instructions, Yes, like that, baby, that's it, she tries to perform as best she can. It's like an operation – you are advised to relax before the first incision. The thin layer of fat she has allowed to cover her body so that she can go unnoticed doesn't alter a thing. He grasps her forearm and hoots, 'Oh shit, I'll have to watch out, you'd easily beat me at arm-wrestling.'

Occasionally Livia gets hold of a copy of the French magazine *Elle* that her mother receives thanks to a diplomat's wife. With the aid of a dictionary, they try to read it. 'The articles talk about the drug problem,' says Livia, 'because in the West they take lots of drugs and sit round in their families watching porn because they're all unemployed, their food is poisoned by all the filth of capitalism, especially their cows' milk, women are paid less than men for the same jobs, and sportswomen are forced to appear naked on TV to earn a living.'

When they go to the movies on Boulevard Magheru they don't

have to pay, Nadia signs whatever receipts she is given. As she explains nonchalantly to Livia, her parents are signing their divorce papers, and she signs everything she can, all the different sorts of cheques in the city.

Recently, Nadia has learned the expression 'we're not going to make a song and dance over it'. She uses it in a letter to Dorina where, in the midst of her comments on the fun atmosphere in Bucharest, she announces that her parents are separating. It was her mother who wrote to tell her this. She feels empty, so terribly split with absences, things already over. And everywhere on sale is the postcard 'Nadia at Montreal!' Perfect. Couldn't be better. What's better than best? So she redirects her sadness, offers it something new: pastries filled with cottage cheese and raisins, fritters with hot chocolate, champagne. Something new, these sleepless nights she recovers from thanks to forty-eight hours of coma-like sleep. She staggers. Steps back, off the beam, her body now a prison rather than a weapon.

But she had been promised she would be freer if she left Béla, and the Federation officials keep that promise: Comrade Coach doesn't register her frequent absences from training, doesn't keep an eye on what she eats, on her new-found friends, or what time she goes to bed. There's no point. In the corridor outside her room a team of 'house guards' take turns twenty-four hours a day.

As if they were inside

The four Securitate agents keeping her under surveillance, the neighbours on her floor, and even the assistant at the grocer's where she shops all agree: Nadia definitely bought a bottle of bleach late that Tuesday afternoon, saying she had to do a wash, even though she had done one the previous evening.

That bottle of bleach. Such a miserable technical detail. No class. No Marilyn Monroe barbiturates here, you take what's available. What you can buy at the grocer's.

For his part, Béla is pragmatic when he mentions the episode in his memoirs, here's the truth: exasperated at being constantly watched by the Securitate, the kid raised a bottle of bleach to her mouth, but it was a gesture of defiance, certainly not a suicide attempt, and she spat it all out in the toilet, crying out, fortunately the agents broke down the door and took her to hospital. Nothing to get worked up about.

Livia, immediately summoned on high, confesses in tears: yes, she suggested Nadia tell the authorities she would swallow bleach if she wasn't allowed to go back home.

The D12 Group in the Securitate officially reports her visit to the hospital where she apparently saw a doctor for 'heartburn' under an assumed name, without him recognizing her. When questioned, the doctor declared, 'What, that fat girl? Obviously not, that's not her at all!'

'OK, I need you to throw some light on this, I can't get my head round it... You've stated recently that the suicide story was false, that in fact on that day you had drunk some shampoo "by mistake", and everyone got incredibly worked up, you included. I'm sorry, but... How can anyone drink shampoo "by mistake"?'

She giggles. I burst out laughing. We move on.

'And how can Béla give his version of what happened when he wasn't with you in Bucharest?'

(I can almost hear her smile.)

'Ah! Béla claims he knows me "as if he had made me". As if he was inside...'

We talk at length about those six months she spent in Bucharest, escaping from her super-powerful body to experiment with a 'normal' adolescent girl's life. I'm waiting for her to raise the episode of her disappearance, a strange forty-eight-hour escape in a Bucharest where a state of siege is imposed while they look for her. I skirt round the subject, she says nothing. I don't insist. I write the chapter. Send it to her. She makes no comment.

And did that really happen? Or is it merely a rumour, yet another one, because there are so many going round now that people know the Fairy Princess is living in Bucharest?

For his birthday, the president of Mexico wants 'the little one' brought to him. Extracts from her Montreal performance, yes, that would be perfect. The deal is done. But she doesn't turn up to the final training session before their departure. Oh, she's not always that conscientious, the Comrade Coach tells the Securitate officials.

Who has seen her? They search the gym, in case she is training in some corner or other. They question the assistants one by one. The young girls in the team. The agents patrolling outside her studio haven't seen her for two days. 'Perhaps she's ill? In bed, unable to answer her phone?' They knock on the door. Nothing. They open the door. The room is empty. They inform the police. 'She can't be found?' the minister for sport and youth exclaims in astonishment. 'Why not dead while you're at it? Don't tell me that brat everybody knows is capable of disappearing into thin air!' The Interior Ministry is informed. The country's borders are sealed. Secretly, a state of emergency is declared, the army searches every neighbourhood in the city. Nothing doing. Impossible to admit to the Most Esteemed Comrade that Nadia has vanished. A sudden indisposition is invented, one that is forcing her to stay in Romania, they will have to go to Mexico without her.

Next morning, she reappears at the airport a few hours before take-off. The Mexican president will get his birthday treat. On the plane, she sleeps with her mouth wide open, wakes to go and throw up in the toilets, then cries and falls asleep again, clutching her worn tracksuit top. It's said the Securitate found her in a fifty-year-old pop star's bed. Or possibly it was a poet close to the regime. If in fact she wasn't found in a park where she spent the night alone.

I decide not to pass on the notes I made from another document in the secret archives that details how, without her, Béla loses it, closes the school at Oneşti and moves to Deva. And how the young coaches laugh at him, this overweight guy who can't even do a cartwheel and who refuses to admit that he didn't give birth to Comăneci, but maybe was simply there on Nadia's path.

He slaps the girls who fall during training, he theorizes, conflict creates champions, he rages, let them fight him, these weaklings! He introduces new rules, the girls must all remain in the gym, he'll bring the teachers from the school to them and put a stop to all that useless coming and going, they will never be out of his sight, not even for a morning. He takes on a woman to search the teachers' bags and pockets every morning, to make sure they are not giving food to the gymnasts on the sly. Until Béla receives a very embarrassed call from the Federation: Nadia is begging him to come and find her in Bucharest, to take charge of her again. He leaves at once.

Monster

'Where is he, the cool Comrade Coach, I want to give him my thanks in person, mo-de-rn thanks, and full of psy-cho-lo-gy!' Béla would enjoy his triumph to the full were it not for all this mess: Nadia has been doing hardly any training for eight months, it's a disaster. The man from the ministry opposite him, one of those who took Nadia away, blinks rhythmically, no doubt out of embarrassment at being forced to appoint Béla as 'Head of the World Championship Team' in place of his young rival.

'However, there is one condition: Our Most Esteemed Comrade wants to see the same girls as at Montreal. He wants Nadia, Dorina: the golden team! Nobody knows your new girls. Do whatever's necessary, Professor, the country is counting on you...'

See the same girls again? But they're dead, those same girls! What little girls? Big fat women with spunk on their cunts who've been lounging around for months! Fucking ce-le-bri-ties! And he's stuck with them for all eternity, 'no doubt until they get their menopause!' he shouts at Márta when he joins her again in Deva. He has six weeks before the World Championships.

Do you want to come back, Nadia? With me?

She cries softly, muffled sounds that give the silence a rhythm. He has carefully moved aside the skirt and tights so that he can sit next to her on the bed. He takes her by the hand, goes over their life together, almost nine years, does not insist on the 10 that for months has gripped her body and throat. 'Baby! Do you know that right at the very beginning, you disappeared? Do you realize you left me the moment I noticed you in that schoolyard... But I always find you again!'

He thought he was lightening the mood, but she weeps inconsolably. Do you want to come back, Nadia? he asks her again; she stays silent, everything is covered with ashes, with endings, with fat, this Illness is like a burial. He is on his feet now, it's as if he is praying.

It will be torture. A massacre. An invasion planned centimetre by centimetre, we'll scrape all that off, discover what's left underneath, if anything. Do you want to come back, Nadia?

When he leaves late that afternoon, he greets the four guards smoking in the corridor outside, and to one of them who asks, 'So, how did you find her?' Béla replies, 'I'll tell you, my lad: last week, during the exhibition, I was told she was in the audience and I didn't see her. Today when she opened the door to me I realized that yes, I had seen her!... But I hadn't recognized her, because... she's a monster, my lad, a fucking huge monster!' and he waves goodbye as he marches off, rewarded for his outburst with loud guffaws.

In her private diary for the year 1978, from which she sends me this photocopied sheet, some words are written bigger than the rest, and are underlined in blue: 'From tomorrow I MUST believe in Béla again. I'm ASHAMED, terribly ashamed of becoming a monster.' And these sentences, copied out several times in neat lines:

'I'm not going to turn my back on what frightens me. I'll face it, because the only way I can escape my fear is by trampling it beneath my feet.

'I'm not going to turn my back on what frightens me. I'll face it, because the only way I can escape my fear is by trampling it beneath my feet.

'I'm not going to turn my back on what frightens me. I'll face it, because the only way I can escape my fear is by trampling it beneath my feet.'

Unable to breathe

At dawn every day he comes to fetch her at the house in the Deva hills where she is installed with her mother and younger brother; she has refused to live in the boarding school with the others. After an hour's run, three hours of light training. Then another run, wearing several layers to make her sweat; then she has the right to a massage followed by a muscle-building session, half an hour in the sauna and, to finish, another run. She attempts some routines on the uneven bars but is unable to stabilize any movement.

'You wanted a normal life, and you've got it, you've become a fat normal cow, and all your fat cells are protesting! They don't want you to be this tank,' says Béla with a smile, slapping her backside so that she starts again.

At night, she cannot walk, and lies in bed unable to sleep because everything aches so much. Flat on her back, she runs her hand over her ribs, impatient for them to stand out clearly once more. Starving, she wakes at four and waits until six before making tea; the migraines she gets late in the evening are a relief because for a few hours the pain lessens the hunger pangs. Everything is as it used to be. For the first days of the training programme, she slept at Márta and Béla's. They have 'set her back on track', salad and fruit accompanied only by iced water, which she drinks in small sips; the liquid trickles down her oesophagus, the transparence of her empty stomach.

If you do as I tell you, we'll get there. Béla knows. He knows exactly what she has 'inside there', and lays his hand on her stomach. The life she led during those months in Bucharest is a distant bank of fog now, reckless nights and rapid sugars. Béla can even foresee the outcome of the World Championships in a week's time. Nothing. Bronze on the bars, possibly, but not on the floor; because to be cute with all that's sloshing around her, these titties, impossible, she is unable to breathe when he puts his finger on her chest beneath the tracksuit top.

Human shape

After a two-month wait, an American television crew receives permission to interview Márta. The young ABC journalist with longish hair would like to call his documentary *The Medals Factory*, the film will be about an hour long.

'Nadia is a metre fifty-six centimetres tall now,' says Márta, handing him some photos that date back to Montreal. 'You'll see her again soon!'

'When?' insists the American.

'When she has regained a human shape!' Béla tells Márta when she poses him the question.

The programme is broadcast just prior to the championships. It lasts fifteen minutes, an enthusiastic quarter of an hour devoted to this marvellous couple of Romanian coaches in charge of a gaggle of cute highly trained little sparrows; they smile for the camera, their fingers raised in V signs, the promise of victory. After the transmission, the American Gymnastic Federation sends a message of congratulation to the TV company, thanking it for having taken their observations into account: this new edit is more upbeat than the first one, the part about Mr Károlyi's methods was unnecessary, and very offensive.

We can send a man to the moon but are unable to teach a young girl to perform on a beam! It is time this country learned how to produce gymnasts who can demonstrate the strength inherent in our national fibre. Since we have no elite national training centres supported by the state, we have to discover what we can take from the Romanian method.

Los Angeles Times editorial, 1979

'Incredible that article, don't you think, Nadia? The Americans up in arms because they aren't living under a communist regime!'

I can hear her stirring a spoon in her cup, without a word.

'OK... in 1981, the United States welcomes Béla, who has fled Romania. Three years later, the American team wins the gold medal ahead of the Romanians. Do you think Béla applied the same methods in the United States as in Romania?'

'Obviously. And he produced champions. There's no miracle about it.'

'But the Americans didn't blink...'

She says nothing. I get the impression she is smiling.

Strasbourg

They say: she's no longer the schoolgirl given a 10 in her gym notebook, a little girl playing with her dolls in front of the entire planet. They note: she has cut off her bunches and stored away her ribbons, her body fills out her costume. They are indulgent: growth is 'understandable grounds for a bit of time out', after all, she has 'caught' sixteen. They count: a gold medal on the beam, a fall on the bars, less speed on the vault, even if she had lost five kilos this summer before getting here. They are amazed: have you seen that Portuguese girl who weighs only twenty-nine kilos!

The young woman will be summoned before them all, gathered stern-faced in the press room. They will expect tears and excuses, she will smile to soften them. 'Luckily I have changed, at Montreal I was fourteen. I am completely... normal for my age.' Then politely, a hostess concerned about her guests' obvious boredom will ask, 'Any further questions?' Then they will notice the blond tints in her hair and before moving on to another interview write quickly in their notebooks one last time, in parenthesis – Nadia C. or the death of a 'fairy princess', while she protests gently, '...I couldn't stay at one metre forty-seven for ever... could I?'

She will say she'll see them again in eight months, in Copenhagen. They will turn up there despite their disappointment. They will go, and they will fall in love all over again. Because she'll be back. The Romania–Russia contest will again be won by the Romanians, thanks to her. Her chestnut hair will be done up in bunches, exactly the same as at Montreal, tied up with red ribbons, a sign. They will almost forgive the kid they once more want to call the kid, in spite of her one metre sixty-one. They will be fooled and moved at the same time when they think of her immense efforts to achieve this veritable comeback: forty-five kilos, four kilos less than at Strasbourg, competitor number 62. She has pulled herself together. On the last day of the competition, she will criticize herself in front of them in a whisper, no, she doesn't touch anything sweet, yes, she has added new difficulties and yes, there'll be more of them in Moscow. They will praise her intelligence for having understood that 'if she went on growing without putting the brakes on, she would have disappeared from the team!' Crowned European champion for the third time in the Brøndby Hallen, she will give the lie to those who asserted that gymnastics was a succession of 'difficulties only capable of being mastered by short-limbed creatures unaware of any fear: little girls'.

Some people will want to spoil the party by mentioning the Soviet Elena Moukhina's exhausted face, only to be told that 'the reservoir of Russian gymnasts is so vast they have infinite possibilities'. What about how thin Nadia is, the hollow between her thighs, her extreme, emaciated pallor? When they raise the problem with her coach at a press conference, he will come up with an explanation. 'It's true, Nadia has lost her baby cheeks, but above all, her features grow hard when she concentrates.'

Interviewed by the BBC, to the question, 'In 1978, you came back into the limelight. Were you no longer a little girl but a… woman?' she will respond with embarrassment, like a repentant alcoholic. 'Yes… That was my… big problem.' Then she will tell of how she went nine days without eating and only drinking water while training hard to lose the extra ten kilos. She will be warmly congratulated on her willpower. She will be applauded and offered a doll for her collection.

Mexico, Fort Worth, Texas

Dearest, I received your last three letters this morning, and I read them like a very sad book of your misadventures in Mexico. Perhaps by the time you get this one, you'll be feeling better!

I saw Dorina yesterday, and we talked of you. She promised she will watch you on TV, you see, she's not angry or even sad that she wasn't selected, actually I think she has met someone! I have to stop now, I have trousers to finish for tomorrow. The apple trees are in blossom, and before, at this time of year, we (the next sentences have been very carefully crossed out, making the words illegible). *Everything here is fine. A thousand kisses to my big girl.*

Mamma

I miss my home. I miss you. Everything is disgusting and it itches. I have got stomach-ache. I'm tired. I sleep even less than at home.

This is how the robot, Madame the Polar Princess, as her mother calls her, goes on complaining for page after page, horrified at being derailed, nauseous as a result of a virus that has hit the whole team from their first day in Mexico. This four-week stay designed to help them prepare calmly at the same temperature and humidity as in Texas, and on equipment like that of the

American arenas, the springy materials that increase the speed of the floor exercises.

Have those glorious months stored up bitter days that suddenly surface all at once? The three months when Béla ratifies Nadia's special position in the team, allows her to choose the music for her floor exercise as well as the abdominal exercises she thinks are most useful. On Mondays, he no longer weighs her with the others, lined up in the gym, dry-mouthed at the thought of the hypothetical grams they have put on over the weekend. He even suggests she train a new ten-year-old recruit. If he's taken to task about the liberties he offers Nadia, he replies that he has force-fed her for so many years that now he only has to let her pour out everything he stuffed in. And it works. Three months during which she doesn't suffer and wins all the competitions. Even hunger and fatigue are nothing more than passing concerns, she has rarely been so sharp, and triumphantly mounts one podium after another. The authorities renew her permission to go abroad without argument.

But what Nadia doesn't write about in the letter to her mother is this feeling that the others are plotting. One morning, it seems to her that one brat is practising 'her' dismount. As soon as she approaches the bars where the skinny little thing is performing, the kid jumps down and strides off nonchalantly. And now there's this virus. Most of them have a fever and throw up whenever they try to swallow any food. In the plane, het up because the competition is drawing close, they yell their results, those figures: less four, less five and, for me, less five hundred and five grams! The kilos lost since Mexico.

On the day after their first public training session in Fort Worth, Béla is horrified to see what the press has written: 'Károlyi's team has lost its enchantment! A bunch of bloodless spiders, mini-vampires from the Carpathian mountains, an army of livid, starving children! Where are the graceful, supple dolls we used to know?' None of the journalists has taken the trouble to add what Béla has explained: they're all so thin owing to a virus. He will have to answer for that to the Romanian Federation and the Central Committee.

Endogenous

It's an infection. Something barely visible a few days earlier, which progresses, settles in. And which she makes worse by behaving as usual as if it didn't exist. Nadia makes a habit of not hearing a thing.

Not hearing when, aged only eight, she falls off the bars and Béla grows angry, shows her a cockroach wobbling its way through the mattresses and whispers, 'It looks like you!'

Not a thing when he calls her a disgusting pregnant cow, a tank, on her return from Bucharest. Not a thing when Béla says scornfully of Emilia, her cheeks sunken from making herself sick every evening, 'Emilia is just lazy! It's easier to do that than have the courage to stick to her diet. Too bad for her!' Not a thing, nothing, not even the swollen ankles of the new girls who beg for their daily dose of novocaine from the clinic. Worse still, she shouts just like Béla at one of the new girls who wants to withdraw after an X-ray has shown a hairline fracture to one of her vertebrae. 'Clench your teeth and keep going, what are ninety seconds?'

She works for him. She spreads his message, she is the living proof of what he professes, the miraculous possible. But now her mission is under threat. After having called the bluff of the Illness, gone through its trials and succeeded in putting a stop to its disgusting bloody symptoms, which her mother mistakenly said were 'inevitable', this is something else: a red swelling on her wrist. She presses it so hard tears come to her eyes, to get rid of the poison. Her wrist throbs dully. Every time the wound rubs against the bar, the injury caused by the steel buckle of her hand-guard opens up again. Bars, chalk and sweat, this mixture is the trilogy of her existence. By the second day of the competition, she can no longer bend her arm. When Béla pokes at it, she groans – she has never groaned before. Do the best you can, sweetheart. He doesn't give orders; he just suggests, he explains calmly to a journalist who is excited by Nadia's performance the previous day.

The warm-up begins. Nadia grasps the bars, tries to balance, but her arm gives way and she falls to the floor. During the break, Béla calls them together in the room reserved for the Romanian team. Our beloved Nadia won't be able to help us, children. He turns towards her, sitting with her arm in a sling, her face wan but her cheeks flaming red – an allergy to the cortisone jabs she is given three times a day to cleanse the blood. Shouts, tears, the little ones have had the stabilizer wheels removed from their bikes, their totem has been stolen. Nadia won't be with us! It's no use him dropping his voice to convince the children of his power. 'You can win! My scorpions!! What? You're scared by those Russian arseholes?' Their chins drop on to their chests, they sob. 'Mathematically, we don't need Nadia, we're several points ahead. And Nadia, if by any chance she was to take part,' he adds, 'had such wonderful results yesterday [they all chorus: Yes, wonderful, Nadia, wonderful], she could fall, several times even, and still win!' Béla lets his words sink in: she would win. If. Or when. She takes part.

She shakes her head. No, not this time, Béla: she shows him her swollen, stiff arm, as painful as toothache. She would like there to be a referee rather than judges, always judges. Somebody who could give her the mark her suffering deserves, and the right not to participate. To end all doubt.

'Are you sure, sweetheart? Really? All right. I understand,' he replies, already with his back to her as he rushes over to the judges. They raise their eyes to the ceiling. Him again. His permanent act, his outbursts, the way he shakes his fists at them as soon as he thinks he has been cheated. His foul mouth. His shows of affection towards the young girls as soon as there are any cameras near them. He hands the judges the list of his gymnasts. Nadia is named for every one of the exercises. The chair of judges is surprised. 'So she is going to take part?' Béla raises his arms to the sky, calls on God as his witness, tears brim in his eyes, his princess is so brave, 'she thinks she'll feel better this afternoon, I know she won't, but what can I do? I've put her down on principle and out of respect for her, as she has given so much to the team.'

The regulation is clear: any gymnast who does not appear is disqualified. However, if she stands up when her name is called and touches each piece of equipment, that means she is still taking part. At each turnaround, Nadia (whom Béla has told at the last moment that he has added her name, 'it looks better') stands up, salutes the judges (just raising her arm brings on a wave of nausea), and in front of all the dumbfounded spectators, sits down again. When she puts her hands on the bars, part of the audience starts to applaud, and Béla comes up behind her and claps, encouraging the public. 'Show them, go on, go on, baby...' until the judges call Béla and the public to order.

Please welcome the incredible Nadia

What is an infection?

The invasion of a living organism by the multiplication of pathogenic organisms. An infection may be either local, systemic or even exogenous, in other words caused by germs coming from the patient themselves. An infection spreads especially when there is a weakness in the organism's natural immune systems. This leads to a struggle between an individual's immune defences and the germs' pathogenic power. Immune defences vary over time and in particular due to many factors such as fatigue, lack of sleep, stress, food deficiencies, etc. The danger presented by a germ is directly related to the number of them infecting an organism. Therefore, an infection will develop all the more depending on how weakened an individual's immune defences are and how intense the infection is.

She is inoculated. Unless she is secreting the poison herself, and has been creating it without noticing for a long time and is weakening from having to fight against herself.

A few days earlier, the team doctor had called it a scratch, there have been plenty of those before, fatigue and stress create the poison and willpower destroys it. Ever since the Illness she has become too weak and porous, soft, soft, soft ever since her time with Comrade Coach, who allowed her to grow so fat she became a real monster, Papa knows how to deal with monsters, sweetheart, fight back! Béla has taught her to fight, while at the same time crushing her ability to fight against anything other than what he singles out. He has delved so deeply into her, calculated, judged. A few weeks earlier, he studied her breasts squashed into her costume. 'You won't have your "problems" this month, baby, don't worry.'

Who is to blame for what happens that afternoon in Fort Worth? The person who makes the decision? The one who proposes the solution? The person who benefits from the decision being made? The one who no longer knows how to decide because she is so accustomed to obeying? Did Béla force Nadia into it? Did Béla offer that Nadia choose between two solutions, knowing that one of them was inconceivable, so that there wasn't really any choice? What is a choice? Eeny-meeny-miny-whose is this body?

Which in the end she offers that day to the packed Texas stadium. They give her an ovation at the surprise announcement that she will perform on the beam although she has withdrawn from the other exercises. The spectators immediately fall silent again, realizing that they are about to witness something unheard of, more exciting than ever: *please welcome the incredible Nadia, who has just decided to… in spite of…*

The bandage on her arm points to the remarkable thing that is about to occur. That is where they have to look.

She takes a deep breath. The flashes, like handfuls of insects thrown into a bonfire, heckle from the shadows and momentarily blind her. A double pirouette on the beam. Stay focused to rewrite. Your legs like paint brushes, sweetheart. Calculating the space and weight of the air as she goes along, reinventing balance.

Now they are completely quiet, twenty thousand silences

that give way to the rumble of her sick blood; a foul taste comes into her mouth, forty-five seconds, half of the total, the horizon scowls at her, without using her hands she thumps the wood with a series of backwards saltos, her bad arm is heavy, immobile, that's it, almost there, she prepares her dismount, figures and angles merge inside her head, think everything through again without that hand, that leap for which she needs to put her weight with both palms on the beam so that she can jump to the floor, this time using only one hand would make her lose her balance, would tip her too far to the right, oh the sickness is palpitating even in her gums and sinuses, she gathers herself and launches her emaciated body horizontally, using only three fingers from her bandaged hand as a precaution.

And she doesn't fall.

Another ovation, her coach carries her off in triumph ringed by her hysterical team-mates, he lifts her high into the light that is so vast and hot that she closes her eyes, head tilted back. When her score – 9.95 (almost the maximum) – flashes up on the board, Nadia is already in the emergency ambulance taking her to hospital in Dallas, where she is operated on under general anaesthetic: the infection has spread all the way up her arm, they are worried about her heart.

When she comes round, she asks for a piece of paper and a pen, or dreams she asks for a piece of paper and a pen. First, note down when it all started: Rodica fell off the beam. What Nadia recalls are a few words from Béla as soon as Rodica is on the floor, something like, 'We're not going to let the Soviets take the title. Can you do it, Nadia, tell me if you can.' Béla, who later writes in his memoirs, 'I told Nadia: have you realised that you have obligations towards the team? Well, you do. Because those little girls don't get any recognition! And how about Márta and me, have you ever asked yourself if you owed us anything? All these years... If you have, Nadia, today you can do something extraordinary...'

What then are we to make of what Béla tells the judges once the competition is over? 'I never asked her to do the whole routine, with all its difficulties! It's incredible! With only one hand... She blew me away, didn't she you?' The judges, who are very uneasy at having seen, scored and accepted the performance of an obviously sick Comăneci.

There are several of them, doctors, nurses and two Romanian officials, round Nadia's bed. She is very thirsty and seems anxious to talk to the surgeon, an American with a fragrance of lemon who carefully separates each word when he talks to her, eager for her to understand how serious her condition is. She takes complete responsibility for the decision, it was a duty, she repeats, 'Yes, that's right, Comrade Doctor, to be an athlete of... for us, in Ro... mania, if you don't suffer, that means you haven't... pushed yourself... to the limit. Nothing her... oic about it but a decision taken on trust Papa. Pa-pa? Nooo... sorry, Doctor.'

No, she continues painfully, Béla did not make her run any crazy risks that day. And as for the 'permanent damage' the surgeon is threatening, Béla had no idea at all, she swears.

They leave the room, and can hear her continuing her monologue in a voice softened by sedatives, 'It's MY choice to obey. YOU always make... me believe I can do anything. Or then... The choice... I don't know how... any more because I'm infested. Sorry, in-FECT-ed.' Later on, she summons the night nurse and asks her to send for her interpreter, she wants to call a press conference, but the nurse can't understand what she's saying, and instead brings her a glass of sparkling water. Nadia giggles when she thinks of the fibs Béla told, his grotesque speech, blah

blah, all you owe us, Nadia, blah blah, all these years. When she would do anything anyway! All services without protection! If I don't kill myself doing it I'm always ready! Papa, I've invented another mount onto the beam because I... My God, it's impossible to finish the story. Next morning, the words she has written are illegible.

'What an imagination! Anyone would think you were with me in the recovery room... Did you know I have a scar all the way up my arm? While I was reading that passage, I thought of something: when I was little and people heard that I trained six hours a day, for them I was a "poor little girl". If I'd been a boy, no one would have felt sorry for me, would they? Do you know that old saying, sport will make a man of you, my boy! Isn't it true of girls? How often do I have to insist to you, I really liked that, I chose it.'

'I think what you're talking about now has nothing to do with what was going on at Fort Worth. It's not a problem. Let's not mention it again.'

Testimony of Rodica D.

'Geza and Béla used to sleep in our room. And if we wanted to go to the toilet, we had to pee leaving the door open.'

'Why?'

'They were worried we would drink too much water and put on weight. What we did was wait before we flushed the toilet, and climb up with a glass in our hand to drink from the tank. They kept their eye on us whenever we took a shower, we weren't allowed to raise our heads...'

'What did you eat before competitions?'

'In the morning, a thin slice of salami, two walnuts and a glass of milk. The same in the evening, but without the nuts.'

'Have you had any serious health problems?'

'Lots! A broken bone in my foot, a broken shoulder and other things as well. I remember that when I got my first period, the nurse gave me a jab and I didn't have them again for a year.'

'...What is this... What is she talking about? We were spoiled! All we had to do was to train. Our rooms were heated and cleaned, and we were fed for free. Anorexia?... Laxatives? Diuretics? Yes, you have to be light to be a gymnast! Accidents? There are some, but not that many. If you count them. So she is "devastated", is she? Honestly, what does that word mean? Injuries? They happen, if a girl is unlucky or hasn't prepared properly. The only time when I... when I didn't listen to my body's pain signals was at Fort Worth.

'I know this is going to astonish you, but it's in the United States that the worst things have happened, because their gym schools are private and expensive, and the girls find they need sponsors and agents right from the start, because there's money at stake. They have to make money to pay off the loans their parents have taken out, they get into debt for years, over there! The investment their parents make, plus their obsession with results... Kristie Phillips says she felt "responsible for her own puberty" when she started to lose because she had grown. Betty Okino broke her arm at a meet because she was forced to train with a suspected fracture so as not to lose the sponsor's money! Kelly Garrison performed with a broken bone in her foot, for the same reason. And their weight was always up and down like a yo-yo. In Romania we didn't go down to the corner shop to stuff ourselves, because there wasn't one, and we didn't have any money! It's true some of our gymnasts took ibuprofen every morning. Others regularly take painkillers on the day of a competition. Is that a good thing? No. Have I ever done it? Yes. Was I forced to? No! I can sympathize with those who feel they were destroyed by the world of gymnastics, but I have no empathy for them.'

'Can I use that, Nadia?'

'Yes, you can. It would be fantastic if they discovered that you don't need to work hard to win, but unfortunately that's not the case. You have time to write that down, oh no, I forgot, you record everything, and here I am jumping about all over the place, sorry. It's not all down to chemistry, you know... Béla thought of everything... For example, we were accompanied by a psychologist, he would make us do puzzles to see how long it took before we got fed up with them, he was testing our ability to persist at something that resisted our efforts. Béla invited passers-by to come in and watch our training sessions; he would encourage them to make noise, to shout, "Nadia! Mariana!" to spoil our concentration. We even had *to do our routines without warming up, in case we found ourselves in that situation one day. We were ready for anything. Monsters!!' (She laughs.)*

Since she knows I am writing this chronologically, she must be aware that we're now coming to the July 1980 Moscow games.

'If you were ready for anything, we can't blame your fall on 23 July 1980 on the groups of soldiers the Russians had put in the stands who were chanting "Nadia fall fall fall" when you came out?'

'What?... I have no recollection of that.'

'Fine... And what did you think when in Moscow Béla Károlyi slapped Melita R. after she fell off the beam?'

'Who told you that? It might have happened, but I was busy elsewhere.'

'Do you think his loss of control was because he knew that if he didn't bring back excellent results to Romania, they would close his school?'

'Excellent results? What does that mean? The things people say... You know something? Some people say that at Moscow I was a failure... Four medals, gold for the floor and the beam, silver for the team event! So? I got lots of letters from people in Romania who accused me of ruining them, saying I owed them a new TV set! They had thrown theirs out of the window because they became so anxious and nervous while they waited for my scores. The things people say...'

'I agree. You were truly extraordinary at Moscow. One theory I find interesting is that by contrast at Montreal in 1976 your innocence – you were still a child, after all – together with your perfect technique in some way infected the judges, as though they didn't dare mess with your score because of your image of apparent purity...'

'Purity? You're saying the row over my scores at Moscow was down to me being somehow "impure" because I wasn't a kid any more? I don't understand. Listen, I'm not sure we can go on. You're

painting everything too black! What about the shades of grey? You're forcing me to judge the whole time. I refuse to judge anyone else!'

With that, she hangs up angrily, and we don't speak again for three weeks. Then I receive a postcard, she is on holiday, and as a postscript, this: 'Béla pushed me a long way but I had worked out my own defence. For example: I knew I could swim fifteen lengths in the pool, but I told Béla I felt I could do ten: that way, I kept five in reserve. He could never break me because he never knew what my REAL limits were, I never revealed them.'

Why does she insist, years later, on denying everything that the others denounce, why not show solidarity, why these stacks and stacks of official versions, why is she so determined to fight, to refuse any notion of weakness, to go on boasting about her incredible strength, 'I never once cried', her constant rewriting of anything that might tip her over into 'poor little kid' territory?

I meet X, a Romanian journalist who does not want to be quoted. In his view, Nadia had a very precise, millimetric self-awareness. The key to her technical superiority was her ability to make split-second mental calculations to correct herself and adjust her sights while she was in mid-performance.

Of course, I'm the one who calls her back, and of course I make no mention of our argument, don't show I'm in any way annoyed. I simply tell her about my meeting. She agrees enthusiastically, delighted to reveal a tiny part of her 'recipe', her trade secret: 'Yes, that's right! I was able to correct myself as I was doing my routine, invisibly: lifting a shoulder slightly, changing the angle of my head, nobody ever noticed a thing!'

'You quietly airbrushed your mistakes... could we say that?'

'Yes, exactly. I rewrite everything! But... discreetly!'

Moscow, in memoriam Elena M., 1960–2006

Comăneci Nadia, the number 50 on the back of her V-necked leotard, strides towards the beam. Pushes back into the shadows the fairies and those old tales of frightened little girls who have to be led so that they don't get lost, victims of their own thoughtlessness. She gives in her notice to childhood and rewrites space with her slender hands, darts like a silken thread and traces a big backwards giant with her foot, inviting bewitchment from their camera flashes, she, the untouchable one. At one moment when she is on the beam there is no music in the hall, she is performing in silence. And it is such a calm expanse, she signs the air in a flourish with her sinuous arms, her hands fly backwards blindly, backwards salto, then a reverse turn. And just as she is preparing her dismount, that thing appears, the thing she mustn't ever think of, in case she is bewitched, kidnapped by the image of the back of a neck crashing into the wood, head first against the bar. Elena's absence merges with it. Elena the orphan, whom her coaches saw as a substitute and who won everything at Strasbourg, Elena who fell a few days before the opening of the games, during a training session. Rumour has it she was forced to get back too soon, before the bone had knit again. Nothing is known about the accident, apart from this: the Thomas salto, her speciality, which she always performed warily (crossing herself in secret behind her coach's back). One day I'm going to break my neck, Coach. No, Elena, girls like you don't break their neck.

Girls like you don't end up in a wheelchair in a bedroom, neck completely fucking snapped, paralysed from head to toe after a Super-E, and it will take a year and then two, ten and then another ten before she croaks on Christmas Eve from the 'consequences of an accident'.

Nadia plunges, her leg tracing an arabesque behind her, a long sigh drawn with a paintbrush. Then, right foot pointing to the front, she turns from all the dead, the beaten, the fractured girls' tears and slowly, deliberately lays out – flip, flap – the bad-luck cards she has defied yet again, she salutes them, they are on their feet, madly in love, overwhelmed at having tasted the terrible smell of warded-off misfortune.

A trial and its biological verdict

'Dear Nadia. You were mmm when you gave that hand gesture at the end of your floor exercise. My mechanical kitten. Nowadays, Nadia is eighteen, she wears a bra and has to shave her armpits,' the leader writer of the *Guardian* concludes in his piece dated July 1980.

This angers people, who does this guy think he is, he's almost sniffing her knickers, really, it's going too far. Whereas it's perfectly normal: did they expect her simply to bypass her biological destiny? 'The little girl has turned into a woman, and the magic is gone,' reads the headline in a French daily, while another proposes, 'From being a big child, she has become a woman. Verdict: the charm is broken.'

What is this magic they are mourning, a hormonal process, this verdict that buries an obsessive dream, a body that, when you used to salute the judges, showed nothing protruding except for the ribs sticking out under the tight fabric. So the change that's been pointed out is a weakness you are incapable of overcoming, an affront to those eyes that caress your downy skin, something never considered in the loving contract between you and the whole planet since 1976.

Moscow, 23 July 1980

We're not going to give the USSR our stamp of approval, we won't go! Offended expressions, heated debates, people talk a lot and very loudly on Western TV channels. Revelations that are no such thing are bandied about, as if they had just been unearthed and there had never been anything so disgusting.

Only a few weeks after the announcement of the invasion of Afghanistan by Soviet troops on 27 December 1979, followed by the announcement that Andreï Sakharov has been placed under house arrest in Gorki, a meeting is held to find a compromise that can keep not only international opinion happy but also the contracts signed by the Olympics industry. Finally, the outline is reached of a patched-up agreement: we will go. But we won't take part in the opening ceremony. We will go. But we will carry the Olympic flag instead of the French, Portuguese or British one, the flags from any of the fifteen nations that cannot afford the luxury of cancelling their myriad contracts and who choose, if they win medals, to hear the Olympic anthem rather than their national ones, which they do not want played in the USSR.

'Where is my doll? Who has stolen my doll?' they sniffle, gathered in the journalists' lobby at the Central Lenin Stadium following Nadia's performance. No, they won't be cheated, they won't have this girl replace the Adorable One. Their disappointment gradually gives way to a bitter anger, she has swallowed the past, the playfulness of that 1976 summer and that 'Ro-man-ia' they pronounced with amazement, unable to get enough of her accent and the way she tightened the elastic on her ponytail, the almost vacant look on her face before she went into action, an implacable toy, always perfect!

They will go through the formalities with the respect due to a once-upon-a-time fairy now being gently pushed towards the exit, the one they no longer know what to call: was it a squirrel? Surely not. Possibly a bird, the albatross with 'invasive limbs' that falls, on 23 July 1980, photographed on the front page of every daily newspaper. The day Comăneci fell. On her back, her hands outstretched towards help that's not coming, a disgraced body bursting out of itself.

She falls one day, but is back the next morning, on the uneven bars, a haughty jewel that forces the computer to play with its decimal points once more: it's 10.00. It's nothing more than one last twitch before the end, they explain knowingly. But here's another 10, on the beam. So she is still the queen, but 'beautiful and sad', faced with her inevitable demise (because that is what has been written and faxed to the newspaper). A queen hastily celebrated before she is finally asked to comply with the verdict on Thursday, 24 July.

A verdict handed down before the trial. A successful foxhunt celebrated too soon, decimal points manipulated by gloved hands that leave no clues, judges fighting over her remains, the last few tasty morsels of an embarrassing body they pretend to evaluate. Because Nadia is out of the picture. She and Nellie Kim, who is twenty-one. The Illness has affected Nellie too, and the Russians have cleaned their team of its stigmata, just as Béla has done: it's enough to keep one girl who is at the terminal phase of her childhood just to show you have nothing against them. New Russian sensation Davydova's nineteen years are a forgivable error, because her hips are tiny and sway as if in front of a snake-charmer, she throws a glance at her coaches, who encourage her with a wink, ninety seconds of teasing child porn.

Last week she calls, at what for me is past midnight. It's about Moscow, she murmurs.

' *...I know you're going to say I no-comment all the important stuff, but for me, Moscow is...* doamnă *[Mrs] Simionescu. And it's my last competition, you know, so I thought...'*

She makes her plea. A little girl angling for me to write the story she wants to read – please please, tell them about Mrs Simionescu. The chief Romanian judge who was also Nadia's first ballet teacher in Oneşti.

'It's not that I want to avoid talking about the boycott... but what did I know about it? We train for the Olympics, we're told the West isn't coming because of the war in Afghanistan. Anyway, back then the American girls weren't worthy rivals, and besides, in Romania we didn't need any extra reason to detest the Russians. What did the West think they had discovered that was so new?'

'But did you know when you got there that it was to be your last competition?'

'No... perhaps to some extent. I was so exhausted. It... went on and on, they kept saying how I had changed. I had known some of those journalists since Montreal, and would have liked to tell them that they had changed as well!'

'That was the last time you were seen with Béla...'

'Do you know something? [Triumphantly.] On the 24 July, he cried.'

Mrs Simionescu

Mrs Simionescu has no proof of what has been going on under her watch as chair of judges, that derisory title which in fact affords her no power. What could she say? That this morning when she came into the room where they have their coffee before the competitions, some judges looked embarrassed? And the speech by the Soviet Federation representative at breakfast did nothing to reassure her, with his 'every Olympiad has its geopolitical imperatives'.

It would be unreasonable to think a deal has been struck. But why then did they keep Nadia waiting for twenty minutes and allow Yelena Davydova to appear first? A stroke of luck for the Soviet gymnast, who avoided the pressure she would have faced if Nadia had scored a high mark. And why did Davydova's score appear almost immediately after her salute? It's as though they had already decided on it while she was performing.

Now that Nadia is on the beam, all she can see are their heads down over their sheets of paper, where they are frantically scribbling. What are they writing? Why?

They are busy dissecting her. They have to find evidence to reach the verdict 'someone' has told them they should reach. For a millisecond, Nadia's long arms flap in the air: did she almost lose her balance after the back somersaults? And was that a slight trembling of her knees when she did her pirouette? Let's put: hesitation.

Maria Simionescu waits for the scores. Béla waits for the scores, calmly. His Nadia was unstoppable. Ten minutes. Twenty. Twenty-five minutes of discussions, the crowd is shouting 'DA-VY-DO-VA', competing with a group of Romanians chanting 'NA-DI-A'. A little man in an official T-shirt is growing annoyed, they're taking too long, he looks at his watch, it's impressively real, you could almost believe in his big, angry gestures towards the East German, Czech, Soviet, Bulgarian and Romanian judges, still with their heads together. Soviet officials, indispensable bit players for the credibility of the scene, come and go with worried looks. By now the whole stadium is whistling. Béla shouts at the public to be quiet, shakes his fist at them, one last act from the crazy madman. Yelena Davydova's coaches quietly congratulate her, she points out that the Romanian girl's score has not gone up yet.

And Mrs Simionescu. Who gave Nadia her first classical dance lessons. Who, in tears, crumples up the pieces of paper they have finally handed her, Comăneci's scores. No, she says to Yuri T., the man looking at his watch, I won't do it, I won't press the button legitimizing this shameful score, this lie, on the board. They cannot do anything if she doesn't validate the result. And there are so many of them surrounding her now, imploring her to be reasonable, people she doesn't even know, Well, dear comrade, well? Hundreds of lenses are trained on Nadia, a row of photographers, their cameras hanging down over their groins, ready to spring into action. White-faced, she stands there side-on, immobile, the Ice Queen who never smiled. The once-upon-a-time kid, facing the baying crowd: the verdict, for God's sake, the verdict.

Abruptly, the little man with the watch leans over Mrs Simionescu and presses the button. The stands immediately burst out laughing and acclaim the winner: DA-VY-DO-VA, serves that Romanian girl right, look how yellow she is, and they point their fingers at the sweating Romanian coach, it's coming out of his eyes, a haggard Béla, who runs over to Yuri and takes his hands in one of his own, How can you do this, Yuri? The whole world is a witness, she was wonderful, you've been an athlete, Yuri, and the Soviet official mumbles some confused words to him, Don't worry, it's complicated, but we'll fix it before the podium, we'll give her a 9.90, something like that, enough to make her first equal. Béla pushes the sunken-cheeked little girls out of his way as he rushes over to the judges, followed by guards ready to restrain him. No one understands anything he says to this woman with a blonde chignon, the Polish judge, who is already packing up and simply shakes her head without looking at him, the crowd is rejoicing, they have understood: the Soviet flag is raised imperceptibly higher than the Romanian one, Béla looks round – my squirrel – his Nadia, the only survivor of a field of Véras, all of whom are now long gone, he can't see her because she is surrounded, they are all at her feet, literally, because there's no more room around her. The little girl who never smiled is crying in front of the cameras and, as if it was a meteorological phenomenon they rush to describe because it might never occur again, the NBC reporter's voice is heard to say, 'She's crying. She's crying. Oh my God, she is crying. All the tears in her body.'

9.85.

All those tasks. Taken in like a good little girl, all their unending demands pour out of her being now, pierced with camera films and flashes, worldwide radioactivity. We're rolling, sweetheart. The great and glorious order of merit of the glory of the great nation, everything crumbles, yes, sir, I see an image of Comăneci crying, her body is a bitterly contested battlefield, disputed and skirmished over, the person whose shadow hangs over Béla, that more-than-Béla of the socialist republic of Romania who in the end is simply another Béla, they're all managers, all of them, they control her gestures one by one, position her so that she will be more efficacious, supple, easy access. Yes, yes, yes, the brown lines beneath her eyes are emphasized by the lights being pushed under her face, now they are crammed between her legs, calling out her name as if she was dying, Nadia, a word, Nadia, a word, a word.

Biomechanics of a Communist finale

Finished, the petrol receipts for his Mercedes paid by the Party, finished too the way that Béla used to decree that the perfume worn by the men watching him stank, demanding from friends at the top that they be got rid of, I choose my security people myself, Comrades, keep your flowery poofs away from me. This morning at Moscow airport Béla is quiet. He climbs into the plane for Bucharest without a curse, couldn't care less about his squirrels. They return home. At the end of the day he is called to the Central Bureau. He is always called in when he returns from abroad, he has to explain to them why he hasn't won gold, for example, or why he has taken his girls to the ballet or a museum without permission, stupid harassment, mere details. Complaints his old friend Ilie V. whisks away humorously, opening his brown briefcase. 'Go on, throw it all in there, I'll bring it back tomorrow morning, washed and ironed!' Ilie, member of the Political Executive Committee and the Central Committee, deputy prime minster from 1978 to 1979, prime minster until the day before yesterday.

Did he call them the 'corrupt games' on the ABC network? Wasn't he supposed to bring back an Olympic title per team? Is Béla losing it? Nadia made two mistakes on the beam and here he is talking about a Russian plot! The truth is they're a team of losers, bad losers. And what about the American press, those dreadful photos of starving gymnasts at Fort Worth, what are they going to conclude in the West, that they don't eat properly in Romania? What about those jokes recorded during a phone conversation on 7 February 1978, when Béla mocked the demonstrations in honour of the Comrade in an 'overt, vulgar' manner?

Béla asks for a glass of water while they continue to list their complaints; never before has he had to beg for a glass of water, With this heat, thirty-eight degrees, it's as hot as the arsehole of a Russian cow in here, Comrades, but they don't laugh, merely look at each other as if his words confirmed a diagnosis. And they keep him there, happy he is so uncomfortable, almost contrite without his 'protector' Ilie V., who has just been sacked from his post on the orders of the Most Renowned Scientist in the country.

End of story, end of the adventure, there is only one date left: 1981. The year when the Conducător decides that sport should no longer be an activity reserved for an elite (a 'Fairy'?) adored by Westerners. The whole country is filled with young, humble working girls who run, dance, skate and jump. Let's start rebuilding on healthy foundations and put the emphasis on popular competitions, 'Daciads', in which 'Everybody can take part, provided they are the best!' Because that's enough of Nadia, Na-di-a, NA-DI-A! Besides, immediately after the ceremony for her return from Moscow, the Comrade demanded some alcohol rub, shuddering with disgust at having brushed against Nadia's cheek; a coating of beige cream and powder slapped on to try to disguise a spot that is nothing more than a mixture of blood and pus signifying a swirl of hormones gone haywire.

'Too many calories!' the Most Renowned Scientist has declared to the world. Nadia's way of life is unhygienic. She is the image of her people: Romanians consume 3,368 calories per day, whereas the Germans only consume 3,362; it's more than time to put into practice the 'scientific diet programme' that the Comrade herself has drawn up as a result of the spot incident. We're going to teach these layabouts how to eat, because if this carries on we'll lose all of our wonderful little girls! The weight of the women of this country, those flabby losers, makes them unsuited to living with the 'strength and lightness' recommended by the Most Esteemed Comrade during his latest TV appearance.

FROM 17TH OCTOBER, BREAD, FLOUR, OIL, MEAT, SUGAR AND MILK CAN ONLY BE PURCHASED ON PRESENTATION OF I.D. AND SPECIAL COUPONS. QUANTITIES AUTHORIZED PER WEEK AND PER PERSON:

MEAT: 550 GRAMS; MILK AND MILK PRODUCTS (EXCLUDING BUTTER): 1 LITRE; EGGS: FIVE; VEGETABLES: 700 GRAMS; FRUIT: 520 GRAMS; SUGAR (INCLUDING SUGARY PRODUCTS): 400 GRAMS; POTATOES: 800 GRAMS. 30% OF FOOD TO BE CONSUMED AT BREAKFAST, 50% AT LUNCH, 20% AT DINNER. IT IS UNDERSTOOD THAT THESE PROPORTIONS WILL VARY ACCORDING TO GENDER, AGE OR ACTIVITY.

Nadia is the one who sends me this list, published at the time in the Scînteia *daily. She adds an explanation, 'It was so difficult, you had to spend so much time checking on what supplies had arrived, setting the alarm for three in the morning to be the first to arrive at the shop and buy whatever you could find, most of the time you didn't even know what you were queuing for, you simply stood in line with the others... You swapped with neighbours. My mother stockpiled food; it's paradoxical, but in those days, people's fridges were full. In the last years we had nothing, because Ceaușescu exported absolutely everything, so then obviously all we talked about was what we dreamed of eating... You'll laugh, but I've heard that kind of obsessive talk over there in the West! All those diets, those recommendations from the Health Ministry, from magazines, they make the same lists as we had under communism! Bah, the state is always worried about what we swallow, isn't it?*

The Katona Dossier

This Securitate dossier on Béla, where the agents 'Nelu' and 'Elena' have noted down everything, including his daily conversations with his wife or his mother. Page after page of absurd details obtained from neighbours, friends, colleagues, who are quite possibly spied on by the people they think they are spying on. Tangled webs of nothing, tightly braiding the breath of every last person, until nobody in Romania dares open their mouth any more.

Why don't they put him in jail? Why in the end do they leave him in peace after the interrogation following the Moscow games? Not only that, but they entrust him once more with the team for the 'Nadia Tour 1981', paid for by the Americans, that will bring in some 250,000 dollars to the Romanian state. This tour during which he is constantly surrounded by 'journalists'. 'Well, big guy, what a surprise, you're a journalist now,' says Béla on the morning of departure to an agent who was already keeping an eye on him back in Oneşti.

It is in November 1976, immediately after Montreal, that special surveillance is put in place on Béla, this 'megalomaniac, braggart, egoist, materialist, who sooner or later will defect to the West'. Agents disguised as sports trainers to keep their eye on him. The moment Béla and Márta leave, they enter their apartment, search it, clothes are left strewn on the floor, drawers opened. As they leave they greet the neighbours so that they will pass on the message to Béla, we'll be back next week to change the microphone batteries. Their electricity is cut off, so is the telephone, they persuade the employees at the Mercur grocery to 'forget' their orders, the teacher is persuaded to find any excuse not to allow their daughter into the nursery. One morning, at the end of his tether, he turns up at the local Securitate headquarters and tries to get his hands on the copy of his keys that they wave under his nose.

Béla wakes up every night, thinking he can hear the microphones hidden in the apartment crackling. He is exhausted. Anonymous complaints from gymnasts, and from doctors as well, accusing him of over-training the girls, underfeeding them, and even of hitting them. Béla suspects all the little ones except for her, not her, but in the end, why not her as well? Sometimes, at the end of dinners he organizes at the last minute to which everyone is invited, coaches, journalists, neighbours, he climbs onto the dining-room table and at dawn, drunk, his arms spread wide, he shouts 'Siiiick!' towards the ceiling, and no one knows whether he is taking to task those who are recording everything, or whether he is wailing in desperation for them to unleash him once and for all.

Filleting the impossible

A few months before this scene becomes real, running along the hotel corridor, knocking on his door, at first politely, then in tears, Coach, please open for me, Nadia gets glimpses of the first signs, without reading them: Béla often finds a stand-in to take his place, he is called to Bucharest 'on business', he receives official documents that he tears up furiously before reading them; Márta silently picks up the pieces.

One evening the two of them are in the empty gym putting away the mats when Béla suddenly takes Nadia in his arms and cradles her for a moment.

She will recount the scene for years as if it was from a film. She ran along that corridor carpeted in dark blue and when she got into his empty, empty, empty room she looked everywhere. Several times behind the doors, even though it made no sense. Béla was too big to hide behind any door, even one in a big American hotel.

She very quickly gets a grip on how the story ends. Refuses to comment on the defection of the person who sometimes, when she was a child, she would call 'Papa', only to cover her mouth with her hand and giggle, I'm sorry, Coach.

On the last day of their tour in New York, Béla confesses to Nadia that he is not returning to Romania. She bursts into tears, begging him to take her with him. He refuses, she is too young, how could he

*guarantee she would have a proper life in that country, Béla writes
in his memoirs.*

*That's false, she says categorically. She was 'trained' (that's the
verb she uses) not to react to anything Béla said, that distance was
an indispensable protection, she didn't believe Béla would leave, so
she didn't cry, she insists, as if it was a crucial detail. Károlyi's defection looks as if it will be a hard episode to unpick.*

*All the sentences devoted to the event in the Securitate's Katona
Dossier start with the phrase 'it appears that': it appears that Béla
suggested to Nadia that she leave with him. It appears that the
Americans helped Béla flee, they had been in contact ever since
1978. It appears that the many purchases the Károlyis made in New
York were intended to avoid arousing suspicion, just like Geza's
call to his wife asking her to come and wait for him at the airport
because he has too many bags to carry himself.*

*In the end I reconstitute a plausible version: at 9.30 on the day
of departure the whole team visits a shopping mall five hundred
metres from the hotel. Béla and Márta are seen for the last time
outside a jeweller's, then they vanish. At noon, three people are
missing from the roll-call: Béla, Márta and Geza. At three in the
afternoon, the Romanian authorities are alerted, it's time to head
for the airport.*

*'These details, all these details,' says Nadia, perplexed when she calls
me, 'I'm afraid they just obscure the essential! How are your readers
going to understand how difficult the decision was for Béla? You
have always travelled with a return ticket in your pocket. Deciding
to go over to the West meant abandoning his family, his friends, in
the knowledge that they would face redoubled surveillance. It was
a terrible decision to take, that sense of guilt... I only understood
what had happened the moment everyone began looking for Béla.
It was as if I was waking up. I ran to Reception, invented some*

excuse so that they would give me the key. His room was empty. It was... the end. I thought he... would never leave. On the plane, the girls were crying, the Securitate agents were in a panic, arguing with each other, trying to work out a story to cover themselves.'

The Katona Dossier ends like this: harassment by those in power, his reputation on the slide after Moscow, and above all the strained atmosphere with Nadia, whom the Son of Ceauşescu has taken over completely, all these reasons explain why...

The Romanian press accuses Béla of high treason, his possessions are impounded, and those close to him, as well as his gymnasts, are placed under increased surveillance.

I have the impression that Nadia was wholeheartedly behind Béla's defection, but she sets me straight. 'He left slamming the door behind him, and all of a sudden I found I was locked in. I was... a prisoner, but in my own country. Exiled. But an internal exile.'

'But... All the same, you must have suspected he was going to stay in the United States, after that moving speech he gave on the eve of his defection to all of you gathered together, when he told you you must carry on working hard, even without him...'

'What? No... Who says that, he does? OK...'

(She takes a deep breath.)

'I've already explained: yes, the night before in the hotel corridor he whispered to me that he was going to stay, but I thought it was a joke, some kind of provocation.'

'Provocation? Did you think he was setting a trap for you like those Securitate agents who claimed to their friends they were going to flee so that they would give themselves away?'

Nadia doesn't answer my question, but lowers her voice because she remembers 'something interesting': a call she receives when she goes back up to her hotel room to get her case (at that moment, no one can find their coaches, they're being looked for everywhere).

'That woman – I've no idea who she was – told me she was getting in touch with me through Béla to know if I wanted to stay in the United States with him, or to go home. I hung up on her, of course!'

As I listen to her, I get the strange feeling that the narrative is being taken away from me, that this story is bogus, I don't believe it, this uninteresting detail is only there to add suspense to a B-movie spy film. She is directing it. She constructs the set and choreographs the actors, puts the finishing touches to their lines. Her own lines are terribly short or non-existent, the part of an awkward fairy who nudges decimal points and sees spectators, judges and presidents bellow as soon as she utters a few words, which are never the ones they want to hear. Like her 'so what?' to Béla when he tries to make her understand that he's never coming back to Romania. The words of a tired adolescent, refusing to feel anything at the departure of the person who sees himself as a father, but whom she prefers to call a 'manager'.

Our versions become entangled, our words vie for the upper hand, Nadia is evasive. Over the next few days, I don't send her anything – perhaps to protect my narrative from her constant attempts to rewrite it. I have only a few dates left to describe, as Romania was completely closed to the media after 1981. I have almost no documentation, and will have to depend entirely on her and her memories for the 1981 World University Games and her retirement from competition that is commemorated with a huge celebration in 1984.

'Do you know that Samaranch awarded me the Olympic Order?'

I reassure her that I will mention her prestigious titles, I'll write about how the whole world celebrated you. Increasingly our conversations, meant to be exchanges, are nothing of the kind. Doubtless it's also my fault, because that day, for example, I don't dare *share my unease with her. What am I supposed to say? I typed your name and that of Nicu C., the 'Son of', into the internet, and found several times the expression: forced 'idyll'. How was I to ask her the question? What is an 'idyll'? What is a 'forced idyll'?*

The Son of Ceaușescu is said to have tortured her. He confiscated her earnings so that she would depend on him. He showed her off to his friends. He wanted her at his beck and call at all times. Stuffed the apartment he offered her full of hypersensitive mikes so that not a single word she spoke would escape him.

The most sordid aspects of the relationship between Nadia and the person the Romanians in secret called the 'kinglet' have been made public since 1989. Unless the version to be believed is that of the kinglet's neighbours, who, when interviewed by scandal sheets, recently declared: Nadia used to turn up without warning to his villa at Sibiu at the wheel of the Fiat he had bought her because she was obsessed by the idea of finding him with other women. She was jealous. Nasty.

Eeny-meeny-miny… whose body is it in 1981? Fought over by Béla and the 'Son of', who demands reinforced surveillance on Nadia. 'I want to be sure she isn't picking men up.'

'Nicu C.?' I write the name without any commentary in a mail, certain she'll refuse to respond. But she calls me that same evening.

'…You know, he was very ordinary.'

'Ordinary? I've read some testimonies and…'

'Yes, that's what I mean. He was the typical pathologically jealous suitor, the sort who follows you everywhere and searches your apartment and your diary. Except that he was a minister and had more opportunities than your average youngster: he had an army and secret agents at his command! He had been obsessed with me ever since Montreal…'

I let her tell me some stories I already know about Nicu C. They've all appeared in the press. In fact, she isn't telling me a thing. And I'm not asking for anything. It's autumn now. Since I took on this project, the frequency of our contact could be represented by an oscillating, absurd graph: sometimes, we exchange mails three or four times a day, but if she doesn't agree with what she has just read, three weeks go by – I'm being punished.

I delay telephoning or writing to her, I'm becoming too aware of her tone of voice, her silences, her reproaches, and at night when I go to bed, I go over her criticisms in my mind, like the day when I express concern about the young gymnasts' sacrificed childhoods. 'Sacrificing childhood? What did I miss out on exactly that was so fantastic? Sitting around in cafés? Going shopping? Going out with boys before I was ready to do so? Video games? Facebook? What do kids do between six and sixteen that I missed out on? If I had lived the kind of normal life you have, what would I be today?'

Increasingly, I am relegated to my 'normal' place, that space she sends me to the way one directs an annoying child to her room to get rid of her. She grows angry, cuts me short, the chapters I send her seem to her 'subjective', she is worried about my clichéd view of Romania, 'Could you avoid expressions like dull clothes, grey streets. And stop reading Geza's views for your book. Remember, he could have been a Securitate informer as well.'

I say nothing and take note. That evening, I watch old videos of her on the beam. Mute, precise, she fillets the impossible the way one might stab an enemy.

When I wake up, there is this brief email: 'With regard to our conversation about Nicu C.: he was never a boyfriend. Really, please don't use that word to describe what happened. Thank you.'

Mechanical fiction

1981–89

The entire country is a film set, everybody rehearses all the time, they no longer know what, but they rehearse just the same. The official text is unchanging, it's as if they were born with it, and besides, they were born with it. It is everywhere. A voice repeats it on the radio, proclaims it on television, it's written on the front page of the only daily newspaper. On every street corner, at work, in the factories, the university and even at parties among friends, some of them become star prompters of the great film, quick to remind you of your lines if you seem about to go off-script. People act opposite other empty actors who look you in the eye, not believing a word, and when it's their turn to speak, you don't believe them either, the words pass through everyone like a bad dream linked to a crazy clock, the words circle around time.

They are performing for two Supreme Spectators, the Most Renowned Scientist in the World and the Comrade, endlessly delighted by the spectacle of a body of which they are the head, who never tire of applauding this country they have imagined and created. In a creaking set full of mediocre props, those empty food stores where the counters are filled an hour before they arrive, the presidential couple shake hands in front of photographers invited to these so-called 'surprise' visits. Since salami, meat and cheese are no longer available, polystyrene foods are displayed. The pair is applauded as they go by, and pretend to be astonished at the abundance of foodstuffs.

But who has ever heard of actors being forced to applaud? When exactly did everything get turned upside down? When did they cease being actors? Unless they never were actors, but spectators forced to watch an interminable show put on by two old ham actors, who are directing their own audience. Everything grows confused. Possibly because people are sleeping less and less as it is so cold in their apartments; a new decree has reduced heating to fourteen degrees, in classrooms it's as low as five. They are also left weak by the lack of food, they have dizzy spells, go astray in their own city, stumbling wretchedly in the stage set that is Bucharest, constantly rewritten and redrawn. People are lost even in places where they have always lived, go up to one another, Excuse me, where is Maïakovski Street? and nobody knows what they are talking about. The streets are renamed, the name of this poet has been prohibited, judged to be too negative: he used the word 'darkness' whereas Romanians are living a Decade of Light, aren't they! A square where people can go in spring is mentioned – what square are you talking about, they insist, you remember, where we had a picnic last autumn; around the table the others point a finger up towards the ceiling, we're being listened to, keep quiet. The square has been demolished, it was old, that writer's statue was dreadfully nineteenth-century, in its place soon there'll be an apartment block with all mod cons. What about the church where we went at Easter? It has been 'transported' stone by stone. It didn't fit into our city, which will soon be a futurist city as modern as Korea's!

She feels dizzy. In the morning, when Nadia is preparing to go and train the juniors, she is convinced she can't face another day.

She will open her mouth and all her stale weariness will come pouring out. All that's left are the gestures. Showing the students how to keep their balance. But the gestures are becoming worn out, too, a mechanical language that no longer makes any sense. One evening she quits the gym right in the middle of a training session. The World University Games are to take place in three weeks' time, she will not, she cannot take part without Béla.

'Why are you so nervous, my love, what's wrong? You'll pull something out of the bag all on your own like a grown-up, nobody will notice the difference,' guffaws the kinglet, 'You just have to end with your backside sticking out, like this, hey, don't be so fucking uptight, don't move.'

Nobel

1982

'Faced with the grave peril of destruction threatening humanity, I, Nadia, we Romanian sportswomen and men, in the spirit of socialist Romania led by President Ceaușescu, that tireless fighter for peace and understanding between peoples, will prevent a new world war, will guarantee peace in Europe and the entire world!'

As soon as she utters this last word, Nadia steps back politely as she has been shown in rehearsal. The Comrade is already in front of her, waving to the crowd. The Most Renowned Scientist in the World comes to the microphone and declares passionately, 'We have to dismantle all the nuclear weapons in the world in the same way as we have defeated Fascism and kicked out the Russians, and we will also...' Here she pauses for effect. 'We will also restore... peace in the Middle East!'

Dozens of little girls rush onto the platform and jump round the couple, singing energetically; in the wings, Nadia is waiting to see whether her services are still required.

Could she have refused to participate in these ceremonies, avoided that pompous speech, for example, aimed at helping Ceaușescu win a hypothetical Nobel Peace Prize? I ask Luca L., a historian. Of course, he replies, just like us, who were no more than simple pioneers. *If we made a couple of mistakes in rehearsal, if we stuttered, we weren't included. All she had to do was fail. Probably she no longer knew how to fail at anything, Luca adds thoughtfully.*

Several months earlier: I send Nadia the passage about Věra Čáslavská, and even though she assures me that she likes it, her breathing seems to me strangely rapid, strangulated, at the far end of the line. 'Are you sure, Nadia, that it's all right?' I insist. Eventually she says very quietly, 'You really like that character a lot... I understand. Věra was so... heroic.'

I always record our conversations in order not to distort what she confides in me. I play back these words several times. I listen to the silence. Her concern that I too am possibly starting to evaluate her precise degree of innocence, and her phrase, 'One can... be a prisoner even when apparently free... Hello... Are you there?'

The hunger circus

Years earlier, when the visiting President Carter wanted to see 'the little girl', the Piața Socialismului was filled with a market. Old women wearing headscarves, their long, flowing skirts stained with mud, sold misshapen sour apples they had picked in the countryside. 'The city centre cannot look like a gypsy village,' the Comrade declared.

Nowadays, the Piața Socialismului is in the centre of a new avenue the Comrade demanded should be 'wider than the Champs-Elysées', even if only by ten centimetres or so. The alabaster-fronted buildings facing onto the avenue are reserved for high Party officials, the pavements can fit thousands of children humming chants and rustling flags. The architects have left room for a covered market. A mirage packed with vegetables and fruit, fresh and cooked meat of all kinds, regional specialities, cheeses from Transylvania and Maramureș – the rare tourists are not supposed to see empty windows. Every morning from four o'clock on, people queue to be the first to buy any surplus, the few items of food put on sale without spoiling the window displays. This place where they come to stare at what they probably will not get to eat is called the museum, the hunger circus.

Romania, the journalist Radu P. explains to me, had become a fiction no one believed in, no one… but we had to go on pretending. The 1980s were a nightmare of the absurd. In 1983, everybody who

· 174 ·

owned a typewriter had to declare it at the police station, and those who represented 'a danger to state security' or who had a police file were forbidden from possessing one! And as for censorship... special Securitate teams had drawn up lists of words prohibited in novels, films or songs. Especially any that mentioned hunger or cold, and were considered a direct reference to Ceauşescu's decrees; you didn't have the right to put, 'He pulled on a jumper because he was shivering'! Everything was read and reread, they even censored the labels on tins. They also invented a new category of persons who needed surveillance, 'people with no police record'...

It was even tougher for us because at the start of the 1970s there had been a relatively open period, when we wanted to believe in a new country. After that... If only we had been invaded by the Soviets, but no, the virus was inside us, we had to fight against ourselves.

I have to admit I find it difficult, Radu adds, embarrassed, to forgive the West for its continued support of Ceauşescu. It's funny, or rather interesting, that it was the right who fervently supported him, like Le Figaro newspaper among others. Doubtless because its proprietor Hersant, like the communist leader Georges Marchais, was an honoured guest at the luxury hunting parties that Ceauşescu used to organize in the Carpathian mountains...

For her part, Nadia becomes coy when I question her about these years, her replies take detours round the back roads.

'I thought of something when you wrote "film sets": the theatres! They were packed; I'm sure I've seen more classical plays than you have! It was freezing in the auditoriums, but it was the same at home, and besides, we wanted to see, to hear beautiful texts... The applause made hardly any noise because everyone kept their gloves on. Obviously there were always Securitate agents in the audience. And Hamlet, you know, when he says "something is rotten in the state of Denmark". I'll never forget that: the actor simply paused for a second after "state"; we understood, we gave him an ovation, we were overwhelmed, he was expressing what we could no longer say. The line was prohibited for the next performance! Oh, and I remember I went with my mother to see Romeo and Juliet; the actors had changed the ending a bit [she giggles]: in the Romanian version, Romeo and Juliet didn't manage to commit suicide because there was a shortage of poison in the country!

'At home, we lived and slept in our overcoats, it was dreadfully cold. We were only allowed fifteen-watt bulbs, the dark yellow glow they gave off was all over the city... I was terrified my mother might fall ill, the hospitals were freezing too and had no way of properly sterilizing their instruments.'

'You see, it's not me who is drawing a picture of a tragic Romania, as you feared!'

She laughs softly at the far end of the line; on my screen-saver is a photograph of Montreal, the little communist who never smiled, then she goes on, 'I detest being cold, it's an obsession of mine even today. And yet despite everything, there are things missing from your descriptions... things that no longer exist.'

'Such as?'

'I don't want people to imagine I am making light of what was going on, but... how can I put it... we were together. Facing a common enemy. We didn't allow ourselves to be trampled on. We had to help one another, get organized – for example, people lent each other their children when they went shopping because they had the right to additional rations of milk and meat. And... I know this is going to seem superficial to you, but all the queuing took so long that it became a great place for finding a date, people put on make-up and perfume before setting out. Old folk met in the lines, they would bring camping stools and play cards. I know these are only details. But... are they just details, or a way of surviving? And *something else you won't hear about because it's not dramatic, but if we managed to get to see a foreign film – it was often French ones, by the way – well, there was a kind of moral obligation to describe it in great detail to all one's friends, we memorized the good bits of dialogue, the costumes, everything, so that we could share that happiness.'*

I ask Nadia whether she can send me a list of her memories of the 1980s, of her daily life. She sighs, *You're incredible, we've talked about it a thousand times, but then, when I insist, she mumbles sarcastically,* 'I won't include my happy memories, I know they don't interest you!'

Ten days or so later, I receive the following:

'Sorry, but they're in no kind of order: the way we collected gift wrappings and packaging from the West, the shinier the better. Cooking at night because that was the only time there was gas. The year the Canadians did a casting to find somebody to play me in the film following my career, I didn't get permission to leave Romania to visit the set. The tins of Chinese mandarin oranges in syrup (everything came from China at the start of the 1980s); watching Bulgarian television programmes even if we didn't understand a word, because we couldn't bear our own patriotic ones any longer; the newsreader would wink and say hello in Romanian! Chernobyl… We were told everything would be fine, that all we needed to do was to carefully wash our fruit and vegetables (but I think that was the same in your country). And something that perhaps isn't relevant, but too bad: I can't understand how people nowadays want to be traceable all the time on their iPhones!'

Breeding killers

1984

We don't talk any more about 'Son of', who accompanies her every-where, like this summer when, against all expectation – when she has not been allowed to compete for four years – she is suddenly authorized to go to the Los Angeles Olympics. She is the brand image of the Romanian delegation that is headed by the kinglet: Ceauşescu wishes to present his son as an ally of the West at a moment when the USSR and most of the Eastern Bloc are boycotting the event, in reprisal for the Moscow games. Nadia is permitted to greet Béla from a distance, but not to speak to him.

I don't tell her that the Romanian journalists I talk to are convinced that these days she is trying to draw a veil over her embarrassing proximity to power by presenting herself as a victim of the kinglet (that's not true, she doesn't claim to be a victim, she says nothing). I am in touch with a university professor, a journalist and even a former Orthodox priest who were living in Bucharest at the time; they agree that of course she is still a symbol, but of what? Too stupid to get out when she should have! Too devious, she profited from the advantages the regime offered her. Remember she gave that famous speech for the Peace Prize in 1982! Too opaque. They all agree, however, that Béla K. always looked after number one 'like an expert, a really smart guy'.

A really smart guy who in the first year after his arrival in the United States worked as a cleaner and a dockworker. Someone who learned English by watching *Sesame Street*, and from his boss, who calls him a red sonofabitch. A really smart guy, who every weekend visits the gym clubs in the neighbouring states carrying in his pocket a pass that never fails: a photo of Nadia. He attends training sessions, takes notes, purses his lips at the dazzled coaches: *no good*.

Two years later, Béla possesses several cars and has his own school.

And they will do anything, these American parents who take out loans to submit their daughters to the judgement of the man who is a discipline expert: a 'commie'. They move houses, change jobs. 'I leave no stone unturned to see what there is underneath,' he assures them, patting the young girls' hair. 'Your delicate little flower,' he hops around heavily, pretending to box an invisible enemy, 'I'll make an anti-communist bomb of her, *we will wiiiin!*'

For a while he is afraid of the unions and the laws in this new country: here, you need a licence to be a plumber, moans Béla, everything is regulated, controlled: does the law prohibiting child labour apply to the forty hours' training the children have to do each week? And the prohibition on minors buying alcohol or cigarettes, he asks the sponsors who are excited by this adventure, do the 'aids' Béla advises come into that category? They reassure him, painkillers with codeine, or cortisone injections, are considered medical necessities. As for the whole bottles of laxatives the girls drink before the public weigh-in, that's their choice, after all, everyone has the right to succeed in life, these little ones have potential, they're miraculous!

The American state remains politely in the doorway to the

announced miracle, on the threshold of the gym where Béla trains Mary Lou Retton, a young gymnast whom he tells the press is 'more powerful than Nadia, a killer', and who goes on to win the Olympic title in 1984.

Who knows?

Yes, who? Who knows why her name is systematically crossed off all the lists? Who knows why she is no longer authorized to leave the country? All those invitations from the West to which the reply is that unfortunately Nadia, who is very, very busy, is unable to come. Doubtless they believe she will rejoin Béla. Whereas she could have done, but came home.

Here she is, stiff as an emaciated doll, in spotless short-sleeved blouse and ankle socks, high up in the stadium, standing beside the flame set into a rectangle of fake marble meant to symbolize a colonnade from an ancient Greek temple, here she is, dressed all in white like the hundreds of athletes who march back from the ceremony at the University Games in Bucharest, raising the torch to the sky, while five hundred children chant in chorus: BR-A-VO NA-D-I-A!

'But how old is she?' the French judge asks the other judges while she is performing her floor exercise to a musical potpourri from her previous competitions. 'The Romanians have gone mad, what is this masquerade, she almost fell after her double somersault, the final salute we've seen so many times since Montreal is absolutely pathetic! And who are her coaches, who does Comăneci belong to these days?'

In the rest area, Maria Filatova raises her eyes to the heavens, exasperated at the cheering. Nadia, meanwhile, takes off her wrist supports without so much as looking at the scoreboard that laboriously shows: one-nought-point-nought-nought, like a doddery old man rewarding his overgrown daughter with barley sugars past their sell-by date. Yet another ten! There is applause – sustained applause for four minutes, as specified in the official instructions, even if for months now – as a security measure – all applause is pre-recorded and every ceremony is lip-synched.

The international media are gathered in the big press room, Nadia is going to make a short statement but will not answer any questions. Nadia is very, very tired and also very, very busy, which is why she will not be taking part in any competitions for a while. 'I am trying. To get some joy from these titles. So they may fill me with fresh strength. Which I need. For… the coming international competitions. That I will participate in. Possibly. Who knows.' She turns her head in the direction of the 'Son of', sitting to the rear, dressed in the latest Western fashion, Levi jeans and a roll-neck beige Shetland pullover. He is smoking Lucky Strikes.

She pulls a light-coloured tracksuit top on over her too-short shorts, the press conference is over, the room is lit up by flashes, pale hiccups, but then she changes her mind and leans towards the microphone, the journalists' recorders bristle back at her again, she hadn't finished! Who knows, murmurs Nadia, who, who?

The menstruation police

W ho knows? Did Béla know she would be 'very, very busy' without him to protect her? Busy, in demand and invited out every evening. The 'Son of' sits her on his lap in the midst of dinners and cocktail parties, moans ostentatiously in front of embarrassed, silent Party members and embassy representatives, jiggles suggestively against her motionless body, Mmm, she's so comfortable, it makes you want to plunge right down into the heart of the queen, oh my, guaranteed comfort, gentlemen, such soft material, let's drink to the sportswoman of the year, who stinks less of sweat now she hardly does any sport these days!

'Nadiiiia,' he croons, twisting around grotesquely and imitating an American accent, 'tell our viewers, if you have a daughter, Nadiiiia, would you want her to do gymnastics like you, eeeh?'

That night she dreamed she was having a baby implanted inside her, she squeezed her thighs together tightly to stop them, and woke up feeling ill, nauseous: she smiles without replying, this migraine, the sun overflows the sky, encloses the atmosphere and her eyes as well, for how many years now have they wanted her to have a child, all of them, she has such a headache, she won't drink again, ever, when she turns twenty-five in November she'll have to start paying the childless-single-woman tax.

Every month, the menstruation police force her knees apart. Push in three fingers in latex gloves. Fingers that search, pinch. No boyfriends? Do you have sexual problems? What date was your last period? When are you going to make up your mind? Have you thought of what you owe your country? Have you thought that you have obligations towards us? Well, you do. Because the Comrade has allowed you to lead a fabulous life all these years. So, Nadia, do something: take part in our country's future.

Illness is an affair of State

As with every head of state, writers used to compose Ceauşescu's speeches. They wrote dithyrambic odes to his glory, and also drew up his most violent decrees. After 1989, they were asked how they could have written these texts while at the same time working on their own books, which they hoped would be easier to publish as a result. One of them replied, 'It's a bit like in the West, those writers who work for magazines or in advertising, for example, they heap praise on products they don't believe in: it was the same for us.'

PREAMBLE TO THE DECREE:

CHEMICAL CONTRACEPTIVE METHODS CAUSE GRAVE ILLNESSES THAT KILL. THEY ARE FORBIDDEN. PRACTISING COITUS INTERRUPTUS LEADS TO IMPOTENCE. BEING SINGLE IS SUSPECT. HAVING SEXUAL RELATIONS THREE OR FOUR TIMES A WEEK IS PROOF OF A NORMAL LIFE. RECOMMENDED NUMBER OF CHILDREN PER WOMAN: FIVE.

DECREE:

ALL WOMEN AGED BETWEEN 18 AND 40 MUST UNDERGO GYNAECOLOGICAL EXAMINATIONS ONCE A MONTH IN THEIR WORKPLACES TO DETECT

ANY POSSIBLE PREGNANCY. THOSE WOMEN WHO SHOW SIGNS OF HAVING HAD AN ABORTION WILL BE PUNISHED WITH A PRISON SENTENCE. WOMEN WHO REFUSE TO BEAR CHILDREN WILL BE PUNISHED WITH A PRISON SENTENCE. WOMEN WHO HAVE CONTRACTED ILLNESSES AS A RESULT OF ABORTIONS WILL NOT BE PERMITTED TO RECEIVE HOSPITAL CARE. IF YOU SUSPECT YOUR NEIGHBOUR OF HAVING HAD AN ABORTION OR HELP CARRY ONE OUT, YOUR DUTY IS TO REPORT IT. HAVING AND RAISING CHILDREN IS THE NOBLEST PATRIOTIC DUTY!

Farewells

6 May 1984

The ceremony is filmed. The countdown on the report about the great gymnast's farewells appears on the left of the screen. The item can be no more than ten minutes in total. Warm golden circles flicker on the scoreboard, then form the letters: N A D I A. The little girls have finished their dance, line up on either side of the person who is preparing to make her speech. She has put on her white tracksuit top after her last exercise on the beam.

She takes the piece of paper handed to her, recognizes the handwriting of the writer who scripts her official speeches. He writes them out in short lines with commas so that she can pause for breath between them.

From today on, she begins. But there is no comma: where is she supposed to pause for breath? She glances quickly at what comes next. From today on. She sees another 'from today on', the text is a litany with no commas, a poem without spaces typed on flimsy, transparent paper.

Five seconds left. She had not planned to be silent for so long, she is simply searching for the comma, she thought she saw it but there wasn't one, her words are chosen for her one last time, the comma jumps from one word to the next, like the decimal point:

one point nought nought, she raises her eyes to those who have no words, they are on their feet, it is as if she is holding the breath of all the fifteen thousand people in the vast gym.

From today on I will no longer compete From today on I will no longer perform. From today on, none of those very special emotions that…

She raises her head, her disturbing gaze stares straight at you until the time code reaches zero seconds, 00.00, her eyes are outlined with a pencil, the air escapes gently from her throat – a slight sigh, she says nothing, it's over.

The only way to avoid misunderstandings, misinterpretations, she tells me, is not to say anything that can be distorted. So I used to stay silent. A lot.

Once upon a time there was a story, the story whose chapters I send conscientiously to the one who is both its actor and its spectator. She notes things, judges them, demands I rewrite certain passages, or applauds. She holds my hand as I write her story, encouraging me to believe and write what sometimes is not quite right, she must know that.

Our conversations become difficult, I come to dread her reactions, I hide bits of my text like the following, even though it is harmless, the testimony of a Romanian woman journalist: 'Back then, in 1986, she was at a loose end, she had fallen from grace somewhat. Ceauşescu didn't need her any more, he was furious at not having been awarded the Nobel Peace Prize. To us she represented another age, the golden age… we were going through hell and she was in the distant past. She came into the newsroom occasionally, we had a coffee together; there were very few articles about her, people were more interested in Aurelia Dobre and Ecatarina

Szabó. *She didn't have permission to leave the country, the official explanation was that Nadia was suffering from "nervous exhaustion". She had put on weight, and people said she drank.'*

And our night-time exchanges too. *One evening when I have just been reading page after terrible page about the activities of the Securitate, and Nadia's continued evasive responses don't convince me, I say I can't believe she didn't witness anything. I insist, probably too much, as though I were dealing with a recalcitrant child. Until she hangs up on me. She calls me back at once, and now I'm the child. I'm so sorry. Forgive me, Nadia.*

'*How do you expect me to... I don't know anything about it! Can you tell me what the secret services of your country get up to? Are they any better? Cleaner? But you know more about Romania than I do, don't you, with all the documents you have... Are you aware that most of the leading members of the Securitate brought out books with their "pseudo-revelations" after the revolution, in order to whitewash themselves and secure posts in the new regime? And that's what you're reading?'*

She rejects paragraphs such as this one, although I have no idea why:

She has a meeting in Piața Universități with Dorina. Whenever they see one another, they only exchange the calm, commonplace comments of day-to-day life. They have to fabricate a parenthesis of normality, to absent themselves from the streets emptied of any passers-by as shiny black cars hurtle down Victoriei Street at a hundred kilometres an hour: the Comrade and his entourage. Not to behave like the others, who ceaselessly talk of the dear departed: paper clips and almonds, hairbands and coffee, What was the smell of sausages with coriander like, do you remember that *sarmales* cabbage we used to cook before Easter? And gherkins with dill in those big barrels in grocery stores and cream cheese cakes sprinkled with icing sugar, stop, I can't bear to think of icing sugar, not that!

It is September, the weather has become warm, bronze and kindly, nothing like the aggressive heat of earlier days. Nadia is seated close to the fountain, groups of students are talking outside the metro station. Some of them stare at her, not sure whether she is the gymnast or not. A quarter of an hour, half an hour. Dorina doesn't arrive. There is someone in the phone box. On the bench, three old women are chatting: one of them smooths out an empty plastic bag, folds it like a napkin being put away in a drawer because it's no longer needed. A young woman points her out to the little girl whose hand she is holding, the child turns round unenthusiastically without stopping. Other students leave the university and come over to the fountain, circles of people build up in the square. Probably they are all carefully making sure they say nothing.

Nothing in front of people one doesn't know very well, nothing to people you are close to, either. But nothing is never nothing enough, and hints of irony constantly arise out of the words one does allow oneself... Like those sly smiles exchanged thinking of a censored, hilarious novel about the two ghoulish Old Comrades, handwritten extracts of which are passed from one person to another (the photocopiers at the Faculty have been too closely watched for several months now). They gather round Dan, who gives a detailed description for all those who weren't there of the American film *Desperately Seeking Susan*, shown in the early hours in an old car park being renovated.

As Nadia watches them, one young girl leans forward towards the glowing tip of a friend's cigarette, her see-through blouse offers a glimpse of her bra, her skin is fresh and trembling, but she herself is there waiting for Dorina, who will not be coming now, and so she will return to the apartment she shares with her mother and brother, all these horizontal days when nothing happens, settling into adulthood.

Then she spots him, alone like her. He seems to be considering who it would be best to approach. Perhaps he knows them. He stands next to them for a while, trying to merge with them, become part of the group, but they shoo him away without even looking at him, and he moves off, scared, towards others who turn their backs on him, sadly aware of his tiny solitude. It's as if it is his first day in a new school, the fawn-coloured dog cannot accept that really he knows not one of them, he carries on searching. Nadia gets up from the bench, she goes off to cry like somebody being sick.

How can I allow myself to make things up so much: she gives me more than enough latitude, doesn't she?

'Besides, where's the interest in it?' she snaps. 'I simply told you I found stray dogs touching, the girl you describe is truly ghastly.'

'No, your anecdote is great,' I insist, so that she will allow me to include this instant of everyday life she mentioned to me weeks earlier, when she was overwhelmed by the solitude of a dog.

I move on.

'I've read that in 1987 people secretly attached anti-Ceaușescu placards round the necks of stray dogs, and also that the actor playing the role of Ceaușescu in a musical comedy was often insulted and spat on in the street. Back then, did you see and understand these signs that something could well take place?'

The moment I utter these words, I instantly regret them. Nadia fled Romania a fortnight before the Comrade's fall. She therefore probably did not see anything coming, even if, the moment her defection was announced in the West, a French journalist claimed categorically that she 'had definitely felt the wind change, she was such an integral part of the regime! She foresaw the arrival of democracy and preferred to get out to avoid having her head shaven' (29 November 1989).

Should this narrative end at the moment when Nadia C. leaves the scene and crawls for a whole night through the mud and ice of a forest in the west of Romania towards the Hungarian border? The flight of the symbol, the heroine, who unwittingly perpetuated the film of the one who in his own way is the manager of Marxism.

Should this narrative end at the moment when the clashing versions of events constantly distance us? Is Nadia right when she frequently reproaches me during our conversations for having 'documented myself too much' and for not really knowing Romania, for not daring to go beyond the prefabricated Western view of a nightmarish communist era?

'If you wanted to write my story, it's because you admire my career. And I am the product of that system. I would never have become a champion in your country, my parents didn't have the means, but for me everything was free: the equipment, the training, the healthcare! Are you aware that in 1988 Romania's Olympic team was more than fifty per cent women, whereas France had only half as many? In the nineties, it was the fashion to hate our past, as if there was nothing at all good under the communist regime, as if we had no past! But we existed! We even laughed. Loved! So there was no flour? That's true. We were all in uniform? True as well. But we didn't laugh at kids who weren't wearing the "cool brand" of sweatshirt, clothes were simply clothes, not symbols! And nowadays people my parents' age are fleeing the country to go and beg in the West, we know how they are received, and it was you who told me one day what "a girl from eastern Europe" means over there...' I hung up before she did. Put the narrative to one side.

'*If you ever come here, we can talk about it, but otherwise it's also possible by email,*' *was the kind reply in English a few weeks ago from a former fellow team-member of Nadia's, the only one who has stayed in Oneşti, the town which now boasts a gym and a secondary school named after Nadia.*

What does she have to tell me, this woman who did not become Nadia C. and who I have succeeded in finding? What is her version of the story? I wrote to Iuliana V. and the few other people I have been exchanging emails with for months now, to inform them that I was coming to visit Bucharest for an indefinite length of time. I was already in Romania when I got an email from Nadia containing a single question: '*Why did you want to write this book?*'

Intermezzo

October 1989, Bucharest

She is daydreaming for a moment, her head pressed against the window of the bus that stops to allow ticket inspectors on board. She doesn't have a ticket, but confidently repeats to the young inspector (did he not hear her answer?), 'Comăneci, Nadia. I am Nadia!' But he doesn't raise his head, and goes on carefully writing down the name and first name of this brown-haired woman sitting alone at the back of the damp bus above the amount of the fine she has to pay. It is his colleague who comes up, snatches the piece of grey paper from him and tears it up.

This anecdote is quoted by several biographers as being the incident that triggered her decision to flee the country.

December 1989, Vienna, US embassy

'It was crazy. Unbelievable. We knew she had fled several days earlier, she had been declared missing. She comes into the embassy, well, a young woman in jeans comes in, with short hair, at first I thought it was a young man. I was on the desk, she comes towards me – frankly, I'll never forget it, I get goose bumps just telling you, I admired her so much, my daughter adored her, after the Montreal Olympics she played at being Nadia in the garden.'

She says, 'I am Nadia C. I want political asylum.'

24 January 1990, Los Angeles, Beverly Hills Hotel

Close-up of her legs in shiny black tights, the heels of her nonde-script flat shoes are worn down. Nadia is playing a few notes of *Für Elise* on the piano. An unsteady circle of eyeliner round her eyes, the fuchsia-pink lipstick is smudged above her top lip. Out of the blue she declares that she would have liked to have been there to kill Ceauşescu herself: she extends her fingers with their varnished nails in a poor imitation of pointing a revolver: 'Shoot! Bang bang!', her brow furrowed.

The journalist waves for her to come and join him on the big hotel bed, and inserts a videotape into the recorder. She shud-ders. Sits very upright, hypnotized by the sight of herself at Mon-treal, this tiny pasty-faced child who on the screen chirrups for the enthralled adults, 'I am Nadia!'

Part two

Onești–București

Night was falling, I had travelled all day from Bucharest in a coach, the hotel where I had booked a room was deserted, each room was as big as a suite. Iuliana had arranged to meet me in the lobby, she lived close by. I had imagined an embittered woman, but she was energetic, warm and pragmatic: everything was prepared, as if time was an issue. On the kitchen table she had opened a book with hand-tinted photographs from the communist era and a photo album crammed with press cuttings following the triumphs of the golden team.

'What is the book you're writing about, exactly? Romanian gymnastics in general, or her? I've known Nadia since nursery school,' she says, pointing to a photograph of the two of them aged six. 'And I'm the first person she called after she fled the country.'

The photo album contained the illustrations for the film I've been trying to reconstruct since I began to write a year ago.

The young Béla and Márta, neither of them much more than thirty, leaning over a group of serious-looking children in smocks sitting on their classroom benches. Béla and the young girls in Paris, in front of the Eiffel Tower.

'That story about the exhibition in Paris, what happened? Did Béla really force his way into the Palais des Sports?'

Iuliana shrugged, then passed me a plate of apple cake. 'The team was split in two. I was in Rome, so I can't tell you anything about that.'

The girls doing winter sports, Iuliana with her arms round Nadia's waist on a sled. At the seaside, each of them holding a ball, pale-faced and scrawny.

'You know – get this down – here, use this pen, yours isn't working properly – Béla taught me to ski, Béla taught me to swim; in other countries if there were things to see, he would take us, he wanted us to learn. He even acted as a tour guide! He was a lot more than a mere trainer, a...'

'A coach?'

'A father. It's such a shame he was bought by the Americans... In Romania nowadays we no longer have the means to create champions, private foundations don't want to invest. We have no more trainers, or the medical equipment to detect and quickly heal anyone injured, like we used to. And besides... who these days would make so many sacrifices for what in the end isn't worth all that much? Our 2004 European champion was forced to sell her medals in a TV show, just so that she could buy a tiny studio apartment; others have posed for *Playboy*... Girls these days dream of becoming top models. We wanted to be invincible. Everything changed when the Wall came down, even for gymnasts... Nowadays they have to wear make-up for competitions, even when they're ten years old. Sequins, lipstick, and their leotards have such low necks, to be more... sexy. Do you remember ours? Not exactly the same style, were they? Have you got enough time to get all this down? Have another piece of cake! You haven't asked me anything about Nadia, is there something in particular that interests you?'

'Yes,' I replied as soon as I could get a word in edgeways. I recited the questions I had prepared during my trip, but they were stale and badly expressed, and she gave responses that seemed to me prepared in advance. There would be nothing to learn or discover.

'One more thing,' I added, a naive concern that had been troubling me for months, 'did Nadia have one or more close girl-friends, who she could share something apart from gymnastics with? She never mentioned anyone to me.'

Iuliana smiled, was silent for a while, then said, 'Perhaps when she was seven, yes. Afterwards, how do you expect her to...'

'You mean she didn't have time? Or that everyone was too jealous of her?'

She interrupted me, waving her hands as if to dispel my words. 'We couldn't be jealous of her, what she was doing was too... far beyond the possible. We were like preliminary sketches of Nadia. I've read so many profiles of her that concentrate on her results, but every sportswoman wants to win! As for her, how shall I put it, she liked to be on sure ground... We are all rough drafts of Nadia, and I'm not talking about the medals... Perhaps that's what interests you as well, is it?' Then, without waiting for my reply: 'What I found extraordinary was that her parents didn't come to talk to Béla at the end of each term. Nadia had to face him on her own. And she did stand up to him. He adored her. Sometimes we had the impression that he was fol-lowing her suggestions, and not the other way round! Nadia wasn't one to please others. When she was little, she was taken to task for it, claimed she was busy fighting monsters and didn't have time to do what other people wanted, I don't really know what "monsters" meant to her! But... I imagine you've been in contact with her, so you know all that.' We stared at each other without saying a word, numbed by the lack of light in the room. She smiled at me.

'You ought to go and see the gym and the statue,' she recom-mended as I was standing up. 'I'd have liked to show you the gym myself, but unfortunately it's Saturday and nowadays the girls don't work at weekends. We used to train seven days a week!'

We said goodbye, she promised to send me the recipe for the apple cake by email.

The next morning, I followed the route she had indicated: the pebbly river, the bus stop. 'We used to be so exhausted after training that even though Nadia lived three hundred metres away, going home on foot was impossible!' A tarnished bronze statue heralded the entrance to the park, with the hands of a young girl bent backwards between grass and sky. Beneath it, the engraved names of the seven young girls, a monument in homage to child soldiers who had faded into adulthood.

The gym looked like a huge floppy tortoise, diamond-shaped windows striping the exterior's flaking blue paint. I walked round it until a gardener came up and asked me to move on.

After that, I spent a week in Bucharest. Met three journalists, two of whom had reported on the Montreal Olympics. A writer, as well. Each of them passed me on to others: 'Listen, I know someone who...' I went to parties, conferences, picnics and bars, people marvelled at the amazing weather for early April, how mild it was. My hosts spoke of my protagonist with respect, what a nice topic, most of them told me stories I already knew. I had no questions to ask. I wasn't investigating anything. I wanted to write to Nadia C., I missed our exchanges, but my efforts at writing seemed too much like the excuses of a contrite, ambivalent lover: I'm not learning anything, Nadia, that you wouldn't want me to know, I'm not betraying you. Contrary to what she insinuated, it wasn't a matter of uncovering the hidden aspects of her narrative, but simply understanding her journey without it being rewritten, including by her.

I criss-crossed Bucharest, with its road surfaces softened by tram tracks, night falling between houses that formed a dark mass barely picked out by the sparse street lights whose orange glow was so dim it was impossible to decipher the uneven pavements. I walked along huge boulevards; the grimy-fronted 1970s apartment blocks ended in a broad square dominated by a giant, almost empty, H&M store. Seated on the ground, an Orthodox priest held out to the passers-by a small dish decorated with fake red, blue and green gemstones; at his feet was a card reading 'Help Me'. The image was so symbolic it was as if it had been deliberately staged on my behalf. I hastened to take notes and crossed the boulevard and was set straight; a maze of calm side streets gave the lie to the certainty of the liberalism displayed in the centre. A sense of shelter. The houses huddling against each other, each one different, glimpses of small rectangular court-yards behind fences often reinforced by corrugated iron, the smell of dead leaves being burned, a young boy beating a carpet hanging on a washing line, a cock crowing loudly. Shops with signs I could not decipher but whose windows explained their purpose: watchmakers, repairers of vacuum cleaners and dolls, barbers, seamstresses, drapers. In the daytime, stray dogs slept in the shop doorways or in the hollows of earth in the flower beds; as the sun went down they gathered along the main thorough-fares where the cars were speeding, looked right and left before venturing cautiously across.

You never told me about the trees of Bucharest, I could have begun my letter to Nadia, in a concrete, anodyne way; here, they poke through the roofs of abandoned houses and grass grows over the grooves in an eviscerated pavement; here the trees spread above their shadows, the foliage inserts itself, takes over. Elms, lilacs, oaks, willows, beeches, poplars and plane trees, limes and horn-beams overcome the space, put an end to time.

You never told me that here nothing is hidden. In the West all cables are buried, façades are restored, everything has to look dolled up, the roads are smooth and freshly concreted; here, whenever a tram goes by, bunches of mysteriously tangled cables sway gently up in the sky.

I wandered all over the city, went to my appointments on foot, fervently noted everything down. The bridge over the Dâmbovița with two metres of missing balustrade with no warning sign, because here its citizens were not seen as fragile: in Bucharest there are none of those flashing signs warning that tomorrow will be hot and that people should drink water; the gaping holes in the crumbling asphalt formed craters that pedestrians stepped round without interrupting their mobile calls. I watched a young couple in front of me in a supermarket queue: he had a beard, and was wearing a Paul Smith T-shirt; she had dyed black hair scooped up in a high ponytail, a pretty, graphic face, intensely self-aware of her absurdly long eyelashes and perfect colouring, her eyebrows redrawn in pencil; her fingers were giving winged caresses to her smartphone screen. She and her bearded companion had already reached the exit when the cashier called out to them, holding up the change they had not bothered to collect. This nonchalant spare change of the new rich in the hand of a bewildered, bitter cashier, as if she no longer knew who the money belonged to now it had been so casually abandoned.

I had meetings in fashionable cafés installed in beautiful Victorian mansions with wrought-iron porches; their gardens strung with multicoloured lights, packed with young people dressed the same as anywhere in Europe. One of these cafés was decorated 'as in the olden days', by which was meant under the communist regime, it was the most popular place in the city, and played only old pioneer songs. From a church squashed between Zara and Bershka, loudspeakers poured out the priest's chant, the tune opening its arms to the street, torn by the sound of noisy engines. Inside the church, red lamps dulled the gold of icons that everyone went along embracing one after another; an old woman brandishing a cloth and a window-cleaning bottle regularly wiped down the glass face of the Virgin Mary. On the table, women in headscarves placed a few offerings, a cake known as *cozonac*, hard-boiled eggs and bottles of oil in plastic bags; a Mickey Mouse bag so full of gifts its torn handles hung down from Christ's forehead.

Old men looking strangely formal, dressed as if for an important evening celebration, stood on their own on the pavement in front of what they had for sale: a collection of Verlaine's verse in French, a set of bathroom scales from the 1970s, the odd battery. Others, the open boot of their car making a kind of stall, were offering crates of carefully arranged fruit, bunches of dill, pairs of new shoes, aubergines, round red peppers, toilet paper, nails. I walked towards what was once Ceaușescu's palace, which seemed close, but the farther I walked, the more distant it became. When I said this to the people I met, quite pleased at my observation, they shrugged their shoulders, they had all had the same experience, that building was immeasurable in size. Why not demolish it? I asked, and they looked at me, annoyed, We have no past because we've silenced so much, said men and women who as children had witnessed its construction, we've already got enough with the older generation refusing to put up with our happy memories!

One evening I got lost and wandered along edgy, nameless streets, zones of unease, with trees piercing the fences and holed concrete; kids watched me like inquisitive dwarfs. When I stopped to consult a map, people came up to help, in French, English, and often we ended up having lengthy discussions without knowing each other. I began to get used to things, to know I was going to hear that in the olden days, in spite of 'all the rest', everyone had a job and an apartment; no one was out of work. Before, there was nothing in the shops, today there is everything but we don't have the wherewithal to buy any of it, so which system is better? They posed the question like a bitter equation. I was shown a leaflet announcing a demonstration in homage to the 1989 revolution.

Back in 1989, did they give their lives so that we would have more Coca-Cola and McDonald's? Did they give their lives for us to become slaves to the IMF? Did they die for us to flee farther and farther from this Romania, a country that cannot offer us a decent life? Die for thousands of old people to sleep out in the open and die of cold? Did they die for the Orthodox church to become this prosperous business that pays the state no taxes? In 1989, they gave their lives for our freedom. That was their Christmas present. What's become of it? What have we done with that freedom? Has it been stored away in some cellar, or are we watching it half-heartedly like an old TV show?

At a birthday party, I said your name and they all sat up as if you had suddenly appeared in your white leotard, still revering that never-to-be-forgotten perfect 10. Late that evening, several thirty-year-old drunken women stood up to launch into a pioneer song they had learned at primary school, embarrassed that they had so much enjoyed singing songs to the glory of the Comrade. A young man with wavy hair sighed *comuniști* for their benefit and hastily crossed himself.

To admire someone who went around with Ceaușescu's son, she was a real opportunist, look at the way she fled thanks to the secret services and left everything behind her, frankly, why devote a book to her? the young man railed without looking at me, while a woman shook her head and covered her ears, That's enough, shut up, you're cursed every last one of you, cursed, daring to soil childhood like that, its enchantment, talking like that about our Nadia, who gave us so much joy!

Around dawn, I asked for the nth time, 'What was it like here in the last years?' In the 1980s when they were all kids; they were so keen to give me their version of things that they kept interrupting each other.

One girl screwed up her mouth when I read out the list of the documents I had consulted, that succession of terrible decrees. 'All that's true. But... we were so sure it would never change that we organized to survive, we developed an internal vigilance, not for one minute did we forget that what we were being made to recite was false. By doing that, we salvaged a life outside the state. Communism? Nobody believed in it, not even the Securitate! Whereas now... they believe this stuff! They want it! They will do anything to join your European Union, they're on their knees in front of holy capital, they get out of work at eleven o'clock at night, and all for what? I haven't been on holiday in six years! But my parents, under Ceaușescu, went to the seaside and to the mountains, to restaurants, concerts, the circus, the cinema, the theatre! Everyone earned more or less the same, and prices hardly rose at all! It was true they were constantly scared, scared someone might hear them say forbidden things; nowadays you can say what you like, that's great, except that nobody hears us... Before, we didn't have permission to leave Romania, but today, nobody has the means to leave the country... Oh, political censorship has gone, but don't worry, economic censorship has taken its place! This pseudo-liberal regime that pretends to coddle us when really it's poisoning us, we swallow it because it doesn't *taste* bad for us, we end up believing in it, but in the end what state does it leave you in? Completely empty! You say communism destroyed our country? But nowadays Canadian companies drive people from their villages and are preparing to blow up our mountains so that they can start fracking, with the blessing of the Romanian government: what a great deal that is! Ceaușescu demolished the city, our parents say? But last night at four in the morning because they were afraid of protesters, speculators demolished an old market, one of Bucharest's historic monuments... and what are they going to replace it with? A supermarket or offices. What is your model? To croak of hunger in the street or to die of loneliness. Boredom in instalments? Struggle–succeed–make it? Make it where? I'm so fed up with being forced to want you, the Western dream, oh, those poor filthy people from eastern Europe who you are constantly teaching the lesson of your marvellous ideal democracy to, OK, we've got it!'

'Write this please: in the olden days nobody wanted to watch those ridiculous patriotic programmes on television, in fact we went out, we lived outside, not huddled up inside in our own homes, we all left for the countryside together, write that, yes, there weren't many things to buy, but really, who needs fifteen kinds of coffee? We used to play music and dance for free, did you get that down?'

They were anxious I should add that side of things, not just the harsh memories of their parents' generation, their terrible version, the ration coupons, the surveillance, the cold, the fear. I noted it all to acknowledge it, the city, the people, the country, the words, as if there was something concealed within it, evidence, I wrote it all down, every shopkeeper greeted me with a '*spuneți?*' (tell me?) which I translated as 'out with it', say what you have to say, I couldn't stop thinking about it, had Nadia said what she had to say, had I heard her? I took note of the country that made you, bore you high like a banner, and which you left on 28 November 1989.

Filling in the grey area

Unless it was during the night of the 26th to the 27th.

Delighted to be offering me the scoop of an unofficial version of events, 'Do you know she simply disappeared from the radar on the 29th and 30th of November, between Hungary and Austria?' asks someone who used to be close to P., who can only be named with this initial because 'these days he doesn't want to talk any more about all that'. This P. whom everyone says was the instigator of the escape, the brains behind it, the one who finally convinces Nadia to leave her country, where she no longer has a future.

She had known him for two years. No, a year. Nadia herself, in the numerous interviews given on her arrival in the United States, says she met him a few months before the great odyssey.

Why make a character out of this man of Romanian origin who has been living in Florida for ten years or more, who, during a visit to Bucharest, meets the former gymnast at a party and leads her to believe he can help her? Usually, nobody is interested in the 'smugglers' of famous defectors. Does this mechanical body always need a manager, somebody to convey to Nadia C. where and how to move, what gestures to adopt? Is it impossible for us to imagine Nadia making a decision for herself? P. fills the empty space, that of a new puppet-master for the once little girl, he fills in the grey area to such an extent that in the end for the world's media Nadia C.'s escape becomes the story of the links she has or doesn't have with P.

When we meet in Oneşti, Iuliana tells me about the call she got from her former team-mate who had been declared missing.

'At first she didn't speak, all I could hear was her breathing. Then she whispered: "Hello? It's me."'

'What did she want?'

'Nothing... I think she simply wanted to hear my voice, a friendly voice. I was in tears, I couldn't stop myself crying... The newspapers had just revealed that she had gone. I was terrified the Securitate were going to catch her, that she would be killed. I kept repeating, Where are you, where are you, Nadia, she promised to call again and hung up.'

In 1989, a French journalist finishes his article on Nadia's defection with these lines: 'Nadia must have called her former team-mate to win her support. As we know, Nadia changes her mind the way she changes her leotards.'

Super-super-E

'*D*on't tell me like everyone else does what I should have said or done back then!' Nadia says irritatedly one day while we are talking about her defection and I have just clumsily interrupted her to ask what P.'s true role had been.

'At the time, I thought that if I followed instructions, if I put myself in the hands of... the person in charge, I stood a better chance of surviving.' She hesitates for a moment over 'person in charge', and when I want to know whether she is talking about the trainers in charge of the team, she is more precise: 'No, it's a general term for the man, the person taking the lead.'

Our conversation ends on a lighter note when we talk about a video of her:

'Those are Super-Es! Extremely risky. Skills that nobody could, or rather dared, to try.'

'No woman at the time?'

'Not one. And no man either.'

Washing away their doubts

How many are there in the entire country who have turned their nights into a secret ritual? Stack the dishes, put the children to bed, then make tea and set out chairs in the kitchen for friends who don't have a radio. Welcome them in whispers, settle down, nothing more than hand signals to pass the sugar, ear pressed against the transistor to find the right frequency, the one for Radio Free Europe, the clandestine station. Occasionally you hear the same crackle of words from your neighbours' flats, and so the next morning you greet them with polite phrases you hope sound warm, we are the ones who listen to the voice. We are the ones who follow the voice, that ribbon signifying a last vital sign for we who are buried, who have allowed ourselves to be buried beneath the tragic vulgarity of the Comrade's national text, those anthems, those 'unanimous' odes to the 'world's greatest leader'.

We have only the night-time and the voice to set things straight, resentful that we don't even dare turn up the volume, dare to budge from the places we have been assigned in this paranoid waltz of silence. All these men and women united without being able to meet, all of them silent nocturnal spectators of the world outside, a world that protest has been chipping away at the edges of for months now. We make our appearance in History from our kitchens, wild with excitement and bitter at the same time, as though each bit of news stirring our neighbours – Solidarność becoming part of the Polish government, the first free elections in the USSR and Hungary a few weeks earlier – only served to reinforce the certainty that nothing will ever change here. We will be in the frozen front row, the leaden seats. We will greet the strides others are taking with respect, that marvellous hullabaloo, those shouts, their tears of joy when, a fortnight earlier, the Berlin Wall came down.

We glance at each other in the kitchen without a word, eyes wide open, trying to imagine for ourselves the Wall literally 'coming down'. We grow frustrated, the voice leaves out so many details! What are the soldiers doing, have they thrown down their weapons? Did they give Mr Rostropovich a chair, a stool? Is it windy? Is it snowing? We listen, heads bowed, staring at the icy kitchen floor tiles, undone with loneliness, crushed by the heroism of these anonymous strangers. We listen to the voice reading out letters from Romanian dissidents that have somehow reached the radio station, hidden inside a doll, at the bottom of a box of chocolates, urgent messages that in recent days have been multiplying and calling to each other.

Compared to all that, in this winter of 1989, what's the story of one last twirl worth?

And yet many do remember the story of 29 November 1989, because, for the first time, the voice made a mistake. It did not give the date or the time, it did not say the name of the programme; the voice came rushing towards them, and without adding anything more, the famous voice of Radio Free Europe announced: '*A fugit Nadia. Nadia s'est enfuie. Nadia is gone.*'

A fugit Nadia. Those who adored her are in tears. It's said that a body riddled with bullets has been found in a Hungarian forest. Or that a woman's body has been fished out of a frozen lake by a peasant. And the 'Son of', who travelled at first light to the border post where she must have crossed in secret, left bloodstains on the walls; no one knows what became of the soldiers.

The kid has gone. With a lump in the throat, people get out old photos cut from newspapers, recall that tune, a charleston that she performed to, the invincible little girl who brought us out in shivers and tears, the kid.

Alias 'Corina' to the Securitate, who immediately start searching for her as far away as Hungary, while her parents and friends, whom she might get in touch with, are placed under renewed surveillance. She had no reason to leave, she must have been influenced by foreign agents, Nadia, that 'popular sportswoman whose achievements are the result of the conditions created by our country to promote the talents of our youth!'

All those who saw her as someone who sold out to the regime are dumbfounded, she rises in their esteem. Just imagine. If she has left the country, someone who after all was in such a privileged position... That's it. Now we are shut in, all alone. Could the last person to leave the country please turn off the lights, people say at the time, sourly proud of the laughter this joke produces.

The hunt: 'Desperate search for Nadia' (l'Équipe); 'Where could Nadia be?' (Le Monde)

1 December 1989

At the centre of her disappearance, she is suddenly no longer there. She deepens her mystery. Just as during those two mysterious days back in 1978 when she is nowhere to be found despite being constantly watched in Bucharest, and no one can discover her until she herself decides to reappear. Trafficking time, trafficking numbers, exploding computers, cursors on the blink. All the documents point to it: there's something not quite right in the story of Nadia's escape. Some things are imprecise, inaccurate, incoherent. I send a version of her flight to Mihaela G.: she left Romania in 1985 by the same route. She returns my text with words underlined, phrases she turns into questions.

Nadia leaves Bucharest on the night of Sunday 26th in a hire car, together with six other people. P. drops them close to a border post, arranges to meet up again in Hungary. But the group gets lost and crosses the border at Mezsgyán at 6 a.m. on the 28th. At 8.36 in the morning of Wednesday 29th, a cable informs the world of her escape. She says she walked for six hours through icy forests, leaving on Sunday evening and arriving in Hungary at dawn on Monday. What is this gap of <u>thirty-six</u> hours? How were they able to <u>rent a car on Sunday night</u> in Bucharest? How could P., who fled ten years earlier, return to his country without arousing suspicion? How could Nadia go unnoticed when she was famous and followed everywhere? It is approximately four hundred kilometres from Bucharest to Timişoara, it's impossible they weren't stopped and checked on the way, especially at night and in a hire car. Where did she get the money to pay P., who was demanding five thousand dollars per person to get them out of the country, when she was earning barely a hundred and fifty dollars a month?

On the 29th, the alarm is raised in Bucharest, the Securitate sets out to find her. At midday, Hungarian television announces she has vanished from the hotel the police had put the group in while they were deciding whether to grant them asylum or not. Rumour has it that she has been snatched by the Securitate. But the hotel employees tell journalists that she left the previous evening in an Austrian car. An unidentified source formally recognizes her in the toilets of a restaurant in Austria. An English journalist, claiming to be her 'secret lover', says he is convinced she has been abducted by the CIA.

At the time, Béla is in Montreux with the American gymnastics team. Obviously he is suspected of being behind her escape; his presence in Europe is a coincidence, he protests. He declares to the press: 'Nadia knows that the best thing she can do is to go to the US embassy in Berne' – is this a message for her? And why, in Berne, did the ambassador stay silent for twenty-four hours before finally promising the press that she wasn't there? To give her time to get out of the country?

She arrives in New York wearing the clothes she stands up in, the ones she claims to have worn 'through kilometres of snow'. What snow? The weather forecast for 27 November 1989 shows temperatures of between minus three and minus seven, a westerly wind, but no snow.

Just as when Nadia was my only interlocutor, the facts overlap until they form an opaque mass: I am told of an officer who apparently was ordered to forbid his men to patrol at the exact time and place when the group crossed the border. Then a former soldier, Valeriu C., states that on 26 November 1989, an NCO warned him that 'very soon' he was going to meet the great gymnast in person.

The last word

There is no doubt, I am told, that the Hungarian secret services were behind it. They organized everything, based on information supplied by Béla K. A team of agents guided her through the forests to the border.

The Hungarians? Obviously not, it's the Americans! It's self-evident that her flight was a godsend for the Western secret services who were trying to bring down Ceaușescu, only a few days after his planned and 'triumphant' re-election at the 14th Party Congress. Besides, the fact that the American media gave every detail of Nadia's flight at the same time as the Malta summit meeting was taking place, where Gorbachev and Bush declared that 'the Cold War is over', clearly shows how the event was manipulated politically.

I dream of her, amused at imagining me stuck in my narrative: how can I move forward without her help, how can I write about that night she spent walking through the mud in the icy forest? She was so irritated at seeing me accumulate all the documentation I could, and would have preferred to be my only source: now she can show me that without her I can't do a thing: I can't narrate how Nadia C. leaves the stage. A perfect preparation for this superbly executed exit, an uppercut, a gob of spit in the Comrade's face. Nadia has just stolen the last word.

A great floor exercise is composed of five ingredients. First, the gymnast must achieve secure landings in all of the tumbling skills. Secondly, she needs good height on her skills, both for high scores and for safety. Thirdly, she has to have endurance because if she runs out of gas before her last tumbling run, she's in big trouble. Fourthly, she must have great conditioning so that she can avoid injuries. And fifthly, she must be able to sell the routine to the judges and audience.

Focus on infinity

The TV screen is split in two. On the right, in a loop, the handshake between Gorbachev and Bush in Malta. On the left, Pan Am Flight 29 is at a standstill on the runway, the grey air makes waves around it, a chilly mirage. The journalists are crowded against the security barrier, where is she, a dot at the far end of the runway surrounded by uniforms, it's her, they shout her name, she replies with a wave of the hand. My God, how hot it was that summer back in 1976, that night when in the press hotel they waited impatiently for dawn on 18 July to see concrete proof of what they had just witnessed, the printed photographs of the girl who never smiled. Electrified by her compact, meticulous body, they had stayed up late in front of the televised replays of her beam exercise, and had woken up from a few hours' rest as if washed clean of their previous loves, completely renewed by her costume, beneath which her coccyx was just visible when she bent down to dust her tiny hands with chalk.

Now they have her in their viewfinders, but she is still too far away, hidden by officials from the Port Authority and the border police. They breathe cautiously so as not to make the image shake and become blurred, this is a historic moment, focus on infinity. There she is. She's holding a red rose in the frosty vapour. She smiles. There are traces of the iridescent blue from her eyeshadow on the lines round her dark eyes. Not especially photogenic, the laugh that widens her rouge-streaked cheeks. She redoes her hair, blonde highlights like blades, then disappears in a swarm of lights and cameras, a snarl-up of commands, Turn a bit more to the left! She laughs. No one has ever heard her laugh. Her lips are pale and pearlescent. A reporter slips a piece of paper to the man clutching her elbow, who must be a cop; he unfolds it in the midst of the scrum and murmurs something to Nadia. She nods and leans towards the mike thrust towards her chest. This brings immediate whistles of protest, boos: the British tabloid the *Mail on Sunday* has just bought exclusive rights to the story she has to tell.

Not everyone can get into the huge room where Nadia gives a short press conference, although she again makes it clear that she won't be saying anything about her odyssey. Who is the person standing next to her? She simpers, hesitates: a friend! Then thinks better of it, no... a manager! They're wearing the same thick faded jean jackets, the same trousers, the same smile over dull teeth, around her neck is a gold chain with heavy links that she doesn't stop fiddling with. A young thug with a rock 'n' roll sneer, her breasts concealed beneath the jacket, short hair brushed back, pearl, neon and hairspray. She's a little boy, oh, the great adventure...

Will she see Béla? Probably, she replies, before carrying on jauntily in English: 'I'm very happy to be in America. For so long now I want to come but there was no one who helped me to do it. I will want a quiet life, but I see this is not going to be very possible,' she concludes, ironic and charming. She leaves the press conference in a patrol car, ennobled by her new status as a political refugee, given to her on the basis of 'well-founded fear of persecution'. On the news that night, Béla K. comments: 'I was scared when I learned she had been seen getting into a foreign vehicle in Hungary, but I was confident, she knew she had to make for an American embassy; now, though, I am worried, very worried! Who is this P. person? Is he honest, and is he helping her find freedom, or is he trying to be her... manager?'

What about her? In her hotel room, can she sense the power of those ellipses in the next morning's newspapers, the funeral odes to the close-ups of her clumsily made-up features. 'The metamorphosis... She gave us so much to dream about. Nadia has... changed.'

The spark

5 December 1989

'Sorry, too many reporters at Miami airport!' she declares after keeping them waiting more than two hours. She goes on: '...my first real press conference in Hollywood City Hall, that's a sign! Do you know something? They're going to make a film of my life! And I'll be in it!' A journalist at the back of the room: 'This is Hollywood, Florida, sweetheart, not California; that makes all the difference when it comes to signs.' His comment is received with applause, whistles, uproar. She turns towards P., who is standing behind her, wearing the same greasy jacket he had on several days earlier when they arrived in New York; their clothes smell of motel bedrooms left in a hurry, disturbed nights, groggy awakenings.

Oh well, too bad, what is the question? she thrusts her fists into her pockets, as if she's in front of the mirror in the hotel bedroom; on the TV screen Madonna defies the presenters with their pursed lips and disapproving looks – *SO WHAT*, masturbation is no crime if you want to be a virgin, cool, if you want to be a whore it's your right – her fuchsia lips are so *SO WHAT*. Ride the wave! Seize the moment! Become yourself! Free, dynamic, ready for all the challenges of this new world, pragmatic and not stuck, her communism dusted off, and...

'I'm sorry, what was the question?'

'Do you know, Nadia, that P. is married and a father of four?'

She bends her head towards them, trembling and pretty. Stays silent for a few moments, licks her lips, nobody has offered her a glass of water.

'What does that matter? So what?'

Two or three things to say to them. The girl whose silence at Montreal had stunned the North American media, that silence she proffered in the face of hundreds of microphones. The way she had of shutting her body off to anything that did not suit her. Later on, of course, she'll talk and talk, oh yes, she won't baulk at reading speeches dreamt up by official writers, this girl who has never expressed herself in public without somebody preparing her text. And it is only at the moment when she decides to put an end to the prefabricated discourse of the Romanian regime that Nadia utters the first words she herself has chosen, an explosion: So what.

So what – cut off: in the hullaballoo they have misheard, what she said was: 'So what? He's not my boyfriend, just my friend.' So what – she only has beginner's English, she didn't understand the question, but answered all the same.

Do I have to trot out all the explanations she gives over two decades of interviews: I knew he was married and had children but I thought that was none of my business, that's what I was trying to say: so what, he only helped me escape? Or is it fairer to reproduce the notes I took several months ago, where she talks of the circumstances surrounding her flight? Notes I took too briefly, thinking we would come back to the topic, annoyed she didn't follow the chronology of her life during our conversations: yes, I too prefer to write her text as I see fit.

Notes on Nadia's flight:

Left midnight. Six hours on foot. Flashlight impossible forests.

ABOVE ALL don't run (they shoot at people fleeing+dogs) walk hands on shoulders person in front not to get lost. Don't think of bullet in back. Concentrate on: staying alive. Lake ½ frozen knees ice anaesthetized cold thinks going to be killed bcs walking behind guy no sense of direction(!) Cross border without realizing stopped 2 hungarian guards she learned few words but recognize her taken away questioned separately offered political asylum she says: all of us or none (gym: team habit?) Hungarian police accept. But H. = Securitate too near, escape Austria next day photo front page newspapers: officially 'missing' in Romania. Split 2 groups 2 cars as far as border BUT: Austrian police stop cars randomly. Cross elsewhere & at night. Concentrate on: staying alive. Six/seven hours on foot, barbed wire fences climb blood hidden flat on stomachs undergrowth waiting P. broke car headlight to identify, then motel, all sleep on floor same room, celebration! US embassy. 'I am Nadia C.' Looked at me like ghost go America quickly/plane in two hours. On some kind of list: people with 'special ability'. Arrive New York after 10 hour flight, press conference. Just left family stumbled icy water darkness barriers barbed wire fences, wounded, unable sleep bullets in back every minute. Prayed not sent back Hungary Austria accompanied man hardly knew, room full overexcited journalists shouting name camera flashes face. In state of shock. Thought get wonderful job, nobody forgotten me people admire me.

Nought nought point nought nought

What would have happened to our conversation if I had sent the following chapter to Nadia C.? Would we have laid the blame on the puritanism in America in 1989? But then what would we have done with the profile that appeared the same year in a French newspaper, of a 'puffy matron who fell from grace once she became a woman'?

Do the little girls who loved her so much watch the prime-time programmes about her where they guffaw: Ceauşescu shaved off everything apart from the hair on women's legs! Nadia left because they wouldn't let her ply her trade, personally I have no objection (the puppet François Mitterrand in the French version of Spitting Image *in December 1989). Do the little girls see the audience tearing Nadia C. limb from limb, what a terrible reverse turn, hordes of little girls witness the condemnation of the little girl who has never once smiled, never said thank you to those whose fury spreads in numbers and centimetres, fury that the object of their desire should have forsaken the spotless costume she wore in the summer of 1976. The fairy whose only desire was to hang gold medals round her fragile neck nowadays gives off a damp perfume, her attitude they say is shocking. True, but 'her appearance is even more shocking!' is the cruel conclusion of a well-known American editorialist. Because that is what this is about: fabrics that are too skimpy and cheap-looking, too much glitter, red lipstick that's too red, careless flesh. Her sin, as the* New York Times *declares: 'she has become like the others'.*

So she will be judged like the others.

Patchwork

*(Los Angeles Times New York Times Newsweek
Sentinel Orlando Times Le Monde Libération
L'Equipe L'Humanité Le Nouvel Observateur)*

She was once a virgin sprite who made us quiver with an adorable wave of the hand at the end of her exercises, her hair
shone like a doll's, nothing in her was like those lascivious, soft
adolescents that Hollywood sleazily serves up: she was a cherub
made of iron, morally inflexible. The little communist who
taught the whole world how to balance on the tips of their tiny
toes shone in our lives until the moment when: she's trampling
on us! It's time for America to kick the Nadia habit. Obviously,
when one sees her, one can't help feeling nostalgic: little Nadia
is no longer little nor, how to put it politely, a bomb one would
give a perfect 10 to. She is a political refugee. They say that over
there they don't have any coffee or steaks. OK, but poor people
over here don't either! We can't welcome all the misery of the
world (especially when it's not really misery, because… a refugee,
someone who *Newsweek* claims lived like a rock star in a villa
with eight bedrooms and servants?) She became a member of
the Romanian Communist Party out of opportunism, she is obviously incapable of any considered ideological commitment. Send
the spoilt, spoiled princess back to her own country, we have
all the avid, immoral bimbos we need here. The Olympic vestal
virgin has become a tabloid tart who uses her desire for freedom

as an explanation for everything and shows no remorse – it's like seeing Cinderella in a porn movie – the slob – trollop – fat cow – trampoline slut – the red concubine, the puffball who dyes her hair – a Barbie fallen into the clutches of a cheap beautician – all that make-up, her childhood nervous flexibility has turned into a flabby maturity with thick legs. The whore of the year, three weeks before Christmas! Thanks for the present! The perfect 10 has turned into a perfect ton, you say goodbye to an elf and you come across a bemused fat lady with faded hair who doesn't understand a thing about the art and ways of creating a good image of herself in our liberal economy. She is worn out, common and rude, refuses to say please or thank you. The plants in her motel room have died, the television is on the whole time, her culinary prowess stretches as far as making an instant coffee. She doesn't seem to have a brain. She demanded to be paid for the interview, it's said that *Life* gave her twenty thousand dollars, or it might have been two thousand. Somebody told me he met her brother in Romania, a skinhead who poured him a disgusting mixture of white wine and fake Pepsi, and showed a video of Nadia's last birthday. In it you can see her dancing with obese, cadaverous-looking military men. She smokes and drinks enormously. Since she's arrived all she has done is eat, drink and shop! That graceful, supple street kid used to drive us wild, but now we're confronted by a woman of a certain age – twenty-eight – with a more than generous bust; everything about her now recalls the unfortunate biological destiny of females, the moment when women prefer to wear comfortable shoes and start dressing in L. In short: Nadia, your scores are very low, judges in America are inflexible!

For your great escape, fighting your way through ice and mud, a high level of difficulty: 8.5. You crawled well!

For your 'Statue of Liberty' pose: let's say 6.5.

For your dance 'I love McDonald's and big cars and God if

you please I'd like a fat contract to pay for all that': 9.5.

For arriving in the United States with your leg over someone else's husband: you stepped out of bounds, sweetheart. Nought.

As for your competition costume, we know you come from the back of beyond, but even so, that filthy jacket and T-shirt with armpits stained white from deodorant, you, the fairy who never used to perspire!

Where you remain perfect is on the ground, as ever... Go on, sweetheart, spread your legs a bit wider and think of America and what you'll be able to get out of the sponsors (even if right now they seem to have put away their chequebooks). Bravo! Yes, go on: 10.

According to the current rules

For a moment, we seem we have lost her, that show-off we loved so much, the one who always escapes, even in extremis, *who flings herself into the void without ever forgetting to salute us first. In an American TV programme a few months after her arrival, she stammers beseechingly: 'I'd like to be able to rewrite everything. What I have said, what I have done, the way I was dressed... I'd like no one to remember my fishnet stockings, my make-up, the blue eyeshadow... I thought miniskirts were pretty. I would have liked somebody to teach me how to dress in the United States...'*

Somebody to teach her. To rewrite her. To absolve her. The little communist bombarded with scores and numbers and words.

POINTS SCORING SYSTEM IN GYMNASTICS:

ACCORDING TO THE CURRENT RULES, THE JUDGES MAY TAKE INTO ACCOUNT FIFTY-FIVE POSSIBLE ERRORS IN THE EXECUTION OF A SKILL ON THE BEAM OR THE UNEVEN BARS. THERE ARE FIFTY-FIVE WAYS OF DEDUCTING A HUNDREDTH OF A POINT FROM 10, FIFTY-FIVE ERRORS TO AVOID IN LESS THAN A MINUTE AND A HALF: LOSS OF BALANCE, TOO LONG A PAUSE, A HESITATION, IMPROPERLY EXTENDED FEET ON TIPTOE, AN

UNEXPECTED GESTURE, KNEES BENT TOO FAR, FORGETTING TO SALUTE THE JUDGES AT START AND FINISH.

Marketability

The mayor of Hollywood (Florida) wanted to offer her the symbolic keys to the city when she arrived, but, 'When I heard that *so what*, I said to myself, "Nadia, you just messed up".'

For Pat R., head of TV films at NBC, she has two handicaps: very young viewers don't know her name, and the story of the love triangle will drive away sponsors. Jay O., vice-president of the International Management Group, which introduces sponsors to gymnasts: 'Nobody wants to touch her any more. She can be forgiven for in the end being simply a woman who dreams of taking advantage of the American way of life, but unfortunately the American way of life isn't kind to marriage-breakers who show no remorse...' For his part, Leigh S., a sports agent, still thinks she is marketable (her escape is straight out of a novel!), and thinks she is still an exciting selling prospect, but Barbara B. of NY Grey Advertising is sceptical: 'Kelloggs and Reebok won't have anything to do with her.' As Vangie H. at the J. Walter Thompson Agency explains: 'We prefer our clients to be as clean as possible, sorry.' Dennis B., vice-president of Dave Bell Associates Inc., a Californian production company that wants to make a series based on Nadia's life, still believes it's possible: Nadia could earn fifty or a hundred thousand dollars per episode. Don M., whose company, Picture Perfect Inc. of New York, is also planning a film, thinks it would be good if Nadia first made some commercials for household names that are also sexy, such as: 'From East to West, Ford!' or a deodorant: 'No Sweat, Perfect in Any Situation!' A famous brand of detergent is probably going to offer her an advertising contract as a result of the interview in which Nadia admitted that her suicide attempt with a bottle of bleach when the Romanian regime separated her from Béla was real. Above all, she has to publicly put a stop to the rumours of adultery. Perhaps a sort of televised confession could be organized, a religious leader from her country could be invited, what are they over there, Muslims or Orthodox? It wouldn't be bad either if she avoided dubious jokes, like the other day when a *Rolling Stone* journalist asked her whether she was an alcoholic. 'Me, an alcoholic? Huh... There's not enough alcohol in Romania these days for anyone to be an alcoholic!'

Despite her tarnished image, the Immigration and Naturalization Service has given assurances that Nadia's refugee status is not in danger, for the moment.

You were not the first

The fairy-master, the boss of the laboratory for little American girls, is invited on to talk shows and interviews. Béla, you lost control of her, didn't you?

Béla: 'Oh, she has always been ambitious, she wanted to reach the highest echelons of the country... she has always had that... ravenous side to her.'

And what does he think of Nadia's answer, as quoted in magazines: 'Béla is lying. I'd like to add something: he was only my second coach, not the first as he keeps on insisting.'

Béla: 'What do I think? Nothing. What does worry me though is that nowadays, with the image she has, she is sullying the sport of gymnastics. Ah, I'd love her still to be what she once was... Fragile, innocent and pure. Now her image has gone down the pan, and that hurts me. My God, it breaks my heart!'

International soap opera

Bobby C., former stand-up comedian, now a lawyer to the stars (Michael Douglas, Burt Reynolds, Dustin Hoffman) immediately saw the potential in Maria, P.'s jilted wife. In fact, he was the one who contacted her. Now, everyone wants her! Larry King, *People* magazine...

'I got her onto the market for paid interviews to guarantee her a living. You have to understand: I'm trying to create a product with Maria because we could hit the jackpot. It's almost Christmas and she has an amazing story to tell!'

'A' side

The camera sweeps round the small living room in the house in the suburbs of Hollywood, Florida. There are no toys strewn on the floor, yellow plastic flowers are prominent in a purple glass vase, there is an embroidered red and black table mat under the empty ashtray. The interviewer, a man of around thirty, clearly separates his words when he addresses Maria P., a young blonde woman with a harassed look who is sitting on the edge of a grimy armchair, four children aged between two and five surrounding her or on her lap. Every now and then she smooths down her hair with one hand, and checks the buttons on her blouse with the other. She replies without hesitation in a monotone. No, she had no more news from her husband after 2 November, when he left to go and visit his sick mother in Romania. 'OK, Maria.

And you saw him again, you learned about everything... from the TV! When you saw your husband as the star guest on a talk show! Incredible! And he was with... Nadia, the famous gymnast from your country!'

'My husband, the man who helped Nadia escape... I was so proud at first, before I, before...' The interviewer leans towards Maria and takes her hand, a moment of communion. 'I immediately prepared the guest bedroom for... her. We can go and see the room if you like. On television, he said he is her... manager as well.' Close-up on Maria's ravaged fingernails, the chapped hands she raises to her eyes as she bursts into tears and the interviewer exclaims, 'Oh my God, my God.' He turns to the camera: 'Mrs P. is crying [her sniffles are heard] because during the press conference, Nadia was wearing... be brave, Maria, tell us, every woman in the country is with you!'

Maria P., her baby clinging round her neck, moans in a very strong Romanian accent: '...she was wearing my husband's chain and his ring!' In close-up, she sobs rhythmically: 'Come home, come home, come home!' The end credits start to roll over a silent image of an ecstatic Nadia C., head thrown back, saluting. Cut.

'B' side

Early in December 1989, a *Los Angeles Times* reporter meets Maria P. His sceptical article appears in the back-page People section, cut to a few lines: 'Maria vacuums an old Buick parked in front of her house, smoking as she hums *Personal Jesus*. She appears relieved to have found a good source of income with this scandal. According to her neighbours, her husband would not let her smoke or go out, instead keeping her pregnant all the time.'

Suitcase

I'm astonished one day when, with Nadia, we look over the completed chapters to find there's no mention of her falling in love, none of those men who might have been 'the opposite of those who played at being managers, like that P.'... Her sudden outburst catches me out, her exasperation: 'I'm not going to apologize yet again! P.'s aim was obviously to become my manager, he told me so in the plane to New York. It's true that I accepted. Because my freedom was worth it, you understand?'

Why doesn't she give me her version of this affair, a twist worthy of a TV film that came to light in the autumn of 1990, a year after her arrival, during another press conference? When she revealed that, in fact, P. kept her prisoner in the United States and stole 150,000 dollars from her that she had earned from interviews. And also that she had known him barely a week when he helped her escape: 'I said I knew him well because he told me it sounded better if I wanted to get a visa. He also advised me to say I didn't want to do gymnastics any more, or to see Béla again. He never left me alone. I had no one to turn to. P. and his wife talked to each other every night on the phone. The scandal was a good earner for them. He used to threaten to put me in a suitcase and send me back to the Securitate in Romania.'

Securities

December 1989

Discovered on 5 December in a black convertible. 'They bought the car on Saturday and paid cash for it: twenty thousand three hundred dollars,' according to Ken P., a Chevrolet dealer.

On the 6th, they left the Diplomat Hotel in Hollywood Beach, where they were known under the names of Mr and Mrs Salders, doubtless through a side door, because they succeeded in escaping the reporters who had been following them for two days. On 12 December, the receptionist at the Beachcomber Lodge and Villas tips off the press as soon as she recognizes the former gymnast, but it's too late: by the time the paparazzi arrive, Mr and Mrs Fonnors's room is empty.

On 13 December, from his room at the Pompano Beach hotel in Florida, P. offers several phone interviews: 'I am her manager and am going to help her make films and commercials.' They live off the interview money he negotiates, the cheques are all made out to him.

Cathy C., a waitress in a diner, explains on a national TV news programme that Nadia 'is like a kid in a sweet shop. She eats five times a day, orders a steak at seven in the morning and a prawn cocktail at eleven; huh, she's having fun like she never could back in her own country... The guy with her? She depends on him to pay, to do the talking. She and I chatted a bit, when he was in the washroom.'

Perez D., barman at the Great Western hotel: 'She ordered a strawberry daiquiri while she was watching *Batman* on TV. Then her picture came on during the news, and she whispered: "This isn't what I was expecting. I'm disappointed, so disappointed."'

Barmaids, waiters, mechanics, curious onlookers, hotel receptionists, cashiers, passers-by, a host of unpaid witnesses, everywhere and always delighted to be part of this fantastic televised trial. Who are happy to note what she eats and in what order as soon as they recognize her in a restaurant. Who scribble down on a piece of paper her car registration number. Who are sure they saw her stagger, drunk, in a casino, or have caught sight of her in a bus, supermarket, square: to them she looked fat and lonely.

Everything was caught on camera, but after being followed by the Securitate for years without ever spotting them, it was refreshing to see who it was who was following me.

– Nadia C.

Fast forward: settling accounts

1999

Hair short and smoothed back, discreet earrings, the ex-gymnast who is the star of the French *Stade 2* programme is wearing a businesswoman's black pinstripe suit, her eyes smoky with taupe-coloured eyeshadow.

The journalist: 'Even so, you were pampered by the regime, weren't you?' Nadia, irritated, in French: 'If I was so favoured, why did I... leave and abandon my medals, my family?' She is interrupted by a Romanian man in the audience who abruptly starts shouting. He can't be heard properly because he doesn't have a mike, but he is pointing a trembling finger at her and seems to be accusing her of something. Ceaușescu's name is audible. She stammers. The journalist invites this unexpected witness onto the set, but he refuses and sits down again, very pale, he seems in distress. The interview continues.

'In 1989, a few weeks after your arrival in the United States, we wanted to do a deal... erm... in fact, we asked P. if we could meet you, he asked for ten thousand dollars, and we refused. P. left for a restaurant with another, erm... client, a Japanese magazine, and so I called you in your room. Why, if you really were being held prisoner, didn't you come down when you were on your own at that moment?'

A sketch flashes on the screen, showing this impromptu trial.

'They're not going to torture her, are they?' Back to Nadia C., agitated, still speaking in halting French: 'You arrive in a country, and know nothing. He told me: "If you do anything, I'll take you back to Romania!" I had fear of... Death! That's why I didn't move and, uh, I've already said the money P. made from me. He does everything to sell me. I was imprisoned in a... free country! [She whispers.] You know... there is never anyone who... helps me. Who HELPS me.' (This last, louder 'help' echoes round the set for a moment.)

The journalist nods, smiles, settles back in his armchair and refers to their previous meeting, in 1983 in Bucharest: 'Do you remember, Nadia? No? You asked me for some chocolate and American cigarettes??? Mmmm... Yes? Well, you can come and pick them up at my place any time you like! We have everything you want here, everything!' (Laughter from the journalists surrounding her.)

Missing in action

December 1989

And so, yet again, she returns to silence to get her breath back: on 16 December she disappears.

'When you've come back to your senses, get in touch!' Béla says sarcastically in a televised interview. 'I expect I'll come across Nadia in a gym competition soon, if she has the money to buy herself a ticket, that is,' the president of the American Gymnastics Federation adds prophetically. When he is asked what she is worth now, the director of a well-known actors' agency replies: 'Her disappearance is undermining her marketability. She has to give something of herself, doesn't she?'

The former communist icon vanishes, but out in reality, her trial continues. At least unless all this is nothing more than a funeral. The funeral for a world, once known as a bloc, protected by a rusty iron curtain. Because after all here in the West, although we didn't love him, we appreciated him, that B-movie villain. That world beyond our own. Implacably better, more rigorous. A boarding school for excellence, their discipline, the beauty of those keen muscles, the brilliance of the red and gold star, the immensity of the dream, a fight between equals, hand-to-hand between scouts and pioneers for almost a century.

Women workers with golden forearms, peasant women

smiling in their flowery headscarves, outstanding chemists with strict chignons, reclusive, persecuted poetesses, sportswomen, oh, the elastic gymnasts, limpid children who are both mischievous and super-strong. All that is dead and buried, now it is transparency, perestroika introducing all those girls who, as if escaping from a nightmare mirror, have turned into the others, into us. Famished whores, wretched, haggard mothers, drab adolescents addicted to the strains of pop capitalism, super-con-artist-businesswomen-models, self-consciously eager to leave behind them a ruined world which, on 19 December 1989, comes toppling down in televised loops interrupted every ten minutes by promises of fresher breath.

Execution

*N*ow comes the chapter there should be no need for me to submit to you. *The one where we are equal, both dependent on what we have read and heard, because neither of us was there.*

I had smiled one day when you told me in all seriousness that in Romania they thought you had contributed to the popular uprising that led to Ceaușescu's downfall; you were a catalyst, your flight proving that nobody could bear the regime any more. 'In other words, you made a supposedly infallible computer system explode, and have brought down a dictator, bravo!' At the far end of the line you whooped agreement, almost childlike in your pride.

In Bucharest, I met some of the women and men who were in Piața Universități the moment the first shots rang out in December 1989. Who had to crawl round their apartments for two days because bullets were whizzing through the buildings and nobody knew who was firing at whom. I questioned several people whose sister died at the age of fifteen, crushed by the tanks.

Others came to meet me, anxious to supply a wide array of versions: impossible to choose only one of them to tell the story of the revolution, they insisted, I had to present the whole bunch. And there were cancelled meetings. Weary refusals to comment yet again on well-known images and the debate: was there really a revolution, or a coup d'état? What precise gesture brought about the fall? And your role, Nadia, in all that, accused of leaving far too late, wasn't that the indication of an escape organized by people

close to Ceauşescu who wanted to replace him and so helped you,
the symbol of the regime, to flee? A load of rubbish, your support-
ers protested angrily. Just imagine what she had to endure with the
kinglet: did she tell you about that?

Seated at a table in a Bucharest café, I listen to the story of a young
woman whose father constantly and courageously opposed the
decrees. Cristina's son is sipping a lemonade, he's ten years old and
is bored until the moment we mention the images of Ceauşescu's
execution. The boy says that when he watches 'the film' he feels
sorry for them. His mother smiles, embarrassed. 'What are you
saying, come on!' The little boy insists: 'Yes, I feel sorry. In the
film, Ceauşescu is like an old grandfather, and so is Elena, they're
trembling and holding each other's hand like dying sweethearts.'

'I'm here, Lenutza,' murmurs the Comrade during his trial,
trying to comfort his wife by using a diminutive. She is wearing
the kind of headscarf worn by the peasants they tried to eradicate
from the country. A banal sign of intimacy between two bewildered old folk who have been torn from their prolonged sleep,
these images travel all round the world. And the two of them
have droned on and on with their propaganda for so long they
believe it right to the end, convinced that all this is the fault of
'foreign terrorists, Libyans, Syrians!', that the Malta handshake
sealed the fate of their country, two model CEOs agreeing on
getting rid of an aged mafioso has-been.

'My children, shame, shame on you,' the Most Renowned Scientist scolds the soldiers tying her up before they shoot her, the
'Heroine, mother, scientist, the living proof of the ethics, abilities
and dignity of the socialist woman, of the Romanian woman' –
the description of her according to the official scriptwriter only
a few weeks earlier. The Old Woman is clutching a small plastic
bag. Nuclear secrets? A list of opponents to be liquidated? No,

the prescription for the medicines the Old Man needs for his diabetes. Their invisible accusers, all those who once had been their zealous acolytes, are in a rush to get this over with, shoot them quickly so that the last members of the Securitate who are still firing at people in the streets of Bucharest will lay down their arms.

That's it. Done. Their bodies are meant to be carried to a morgue by strong volunteers: a soldier who is a champion canoeist, another who is a rugby player, soccer and hockey champion, but on 25 December 1989 the bodies are nowhere to be found. No sign of them in the stadium where it was thought they had been left; they have vanished into thin air. Until the morning of the 26th, when they are discovered in a different stadium. Who has moved them? Why? Inconsistencies, hearsay, odd details: when the death sentence is pronounced, the journalists think the execution is going to take place later that evening or the next day. The cameraman switches off his camera at the very moment when the volley of shots rings out in the courtyard. All he can film are the two bullet-riddled bodies on the ground. Barely fifteen minutes have elapsed between sentencing and execution.

Hello, who's there?

Thursday, 21 December 1989

They know. Both sides, those who have been giving orders for years, and those who have obeyed them. All of them dependent every night on the voice of Radio Free Europe: no, they are not giving way, those silhouettes huddled in the depths of the Timişoara night, frozen stiff, demanding the return of the pastor whom Ceauşescu has just sentenced to house arrest, suspected of giving 'subversive sermons'.

More than a thousand of them in that big square, most of them born as a result of Decree 770, born from failed abortions; at most they possess three guns, possibly four, and yet they advance towards the soldiers who have their rifles levelled at them. Fire at will, commands the kinglet when he hears: we're in a state of war! What war? They're already dead, killed at point-blank range. So then we'll go on strike, the survivors decide.

In Bucharest they know too, those hand-picked workers pushed forward by the Securitate agents, quick, we have to fill this bus leaving from the factory to go and applaud the speech by the man they have nicknamed The Hateful One, a rapidly thrown-together speech to demonstrate his authority in the face of recent events.

And here it resonates, that echo of the bodies people stumble over in the streets of Timişoara, and here they hear it, those men crammed into the bus. They have to do something. During the journey to the centre of Bucharest, they whisper to one another as discreetly as possible: what can they do? Jump off as it goes along, persuade the driver to stop? Impossible, they are surrounded by vans full of the usual accessories, the blue–yellow–red flags, banners proclaiming the Comrade's glory. All right, if they have to be part of the spectacle yet again, they will boo him, they will tear at the silence constructed thanks to the horror they've had rammed down their throats and into their brains for years now.

About twenty of them reach an agreement. They will shout: Timişoara. Staggered by their decision, stomachs churning, they fall silent and look out of the bus windows at the capital's deserted streets. All the workers from the Bucharest factories are already in Palace Square, the pioneers at the front, flanked by important Party members. The platform is protected by rows of police. Guards are watching the surrounding streets. Securitate agents are posted everywhere among the crowd.

How do they do it? Do they take a deep breath before they launch themselves, or on the contrary, do they block out everything, fear, breathing, everything they should not think of? A Super-super-E. Let the air filter into their loosened throats, clench their abdomens, turn the ribcage into an echo chamber, and, almost inaudibly among the obligatory 'Hurrah CE-AU-ŞES-CU!', let out a feeble: ti-mi-şo-a-ra, ti-mi-şo-a-ra.

A few gasps escape from the stupefied bodies around them. A quiver, followed by nothing. An interruption. Up on the platform, the Comrade, an aged silhouette in black coat and astrakhan hat, has stopped speaking. Stunned. He turns to his wife, to his frozen ministers.

And there are only two left out of the twenty workers who swore on the bus that they would do something, two who are still holding the blue–yellow–red flags they have been told to wave.

And they step forward, where are they going, no idea, they move slowly forward in the midst of the bewildered crowd, ti-mi-șo-a-ra ti-mi-șo-a-ra. The Old Man clears his throat, taps the mike as if it is an old, out-of-order telephone receiver, there must be some technical problem – get back to the point – what was he saying, oh yes, the terrorist menace threatening the country, the foreign agents who had come to create chaos in Timișoara – Romania condemns this a-ggress-ion – we will re-establish order and the – above all don't think about – the Wall – Rostropovich – the Bulgarians Poland Germany – a handshake, transparency, he says, that other Russian manager of – he is feeling giddy. Licks his dry lips.

HE-LLO? He questions the December wind, sprinkled with distant cries: ti-mi-șo-a-ra ti-mi-șo-a-ra. Hello? Hello? Who's there? Who are you? Who is it? Who knows. He seems to see a wave at the back of the crowd, the sun is shining, violent and icy, is it a new dance the children are performing, or what? The Most Renowned Scientist in the World grasps his arm, whispers lines he doesn't know, what is she talking about, Promise them a wage rise, she repeats, a schoolmarm who can no longer control the crowd, HELL-O, she shouts, but far from the microphone her silly voice croaks, silence, be quiet, eh, silence be quiet, eh that's enough who's there, and he, the Old Man, is like a scratched record, gets stuck, groans hello hello hello hell-o hello *So What*. It's finished. The image freezes, the televised retransmission is interrupted by a patriotic song over a shaky test card.

Then the special broadcast resumes: beneath a soft blue sky, a scantily dressed crowd gathers round the platform. They had to act quickly to find some images and to be able to continue the narrative come what may: they come from a meeting the previous summer.

At what moment is everything turned upside down? What is

the event that transforms these eternal spectators into actors? A few brave people shout 'Timișoara', then almost at once an explosion produces a mass exit and everyone flees the square, scattering, turning their backs on the Comrade without receiving his permission, something unheard of. But what is this explosion? Nothing more than a firecracker thrown by the workers determined to put an end to things? A diversion by the regime to cover the slogans hostile to Ceaușescu? The noise of tanks moving along the nearby boulevards to contain the first opponents, a small group of demonstrators who are already trying to storm the palace? And the following day, who fires at the small crowd that for the first time gathers of its own accord? Almost a thousand dead in a few days for a non-velvet revolution. Impossible to imagine they are all ricochets from stray bullets, I am told in Bucharest. So where do these bursts of fire come from? From those mythical gangs of psychotic orphans, Ceaușescu's last supporters, trained since childhood to venerate and protect him? Soviet agents, those tourists who had flooded into the country from the start of December? Who is directing the snipers? Who is shooting at whom? Everyone is shooting at everyone, because for decades nobody has known who is who. Who to trust.

Numbers: 13-95-25

Calls recorded between 25 and 26 December to 13-95-25, the answering machine of Romanian state television, which the revolutionaries have taken over, at a moment when, although the execution of the Ceauşescus has been announced, no image of it has yet been broadcast.

'Hello? I'm the mother of a twenty-one-year-old soldier [sobs]. I, I don't have any news of him. Is there a list of the wounded anywhere? Of the... dead?'

'Hello? Hello? Show yourselves on screen at least! Who are you? We want to see images of the execution. The film. Details.'

'Hello? I want news of the Com... I mean the ex-Comrade.'

'Hello? Listen: my brother is in the Securitate. He doesn't have a weapon, he never has had, why do you all talk of them as if they were the devil? It's not true, not true!'

'Hello? I want to see. Everything. We want to see everything.'

'Hello, censorship was abolished three days ago, and you, you [he shouts]. Why do we still have to stay calm and patient, eh?' (He sobs.)

'Hello, all right: my wife disappeared two days ago. Please, look for her. In the hospitals, everywhere! She must be a... a... an accomplice. Of those terrorists, the Securitate, give everyone her details! Arrest her!'

(Furious, she declaims) 'Are we being cheated yet again? We're going to, we're going to put a bomb. We women are, we've always been under the yoke of others; the Romania of obedient bodies is dead, sir!'

'Hello? Hello, can you hear me? Ha, it's an answering machine... from the depths of our hearts, the depths of our souls, we beg you, we want to see the criminal, we want to judge him ourselves, don't do it...'

Messages recorded on the same answering machine the following day, after the broadcast showing the dead bodies of the Ceauşescus.

'Hello, I have a question: why does the body have light-coloured eyes when in fact they were dark? Hmm?'

(Exhausted) 'Listen to me... We... have... film directors. We... have... actors. We have... a ... champion. We could... make a... film of all that period, our... the life of that filthy guy, of us.'

They rush in a disorderly fashion towards the building that houses Romanian state television. Thousands, in the freezing night, chanting and demanding over and over until dawn: *A DE VĂ RUL A DE VĂ RUL A DE VĂ RUL* (the truth the truth the truth).

There in the West they know the truth. Oh, the romantic version was fascinating for a few days, let's say until 24 December 1989, Christmas Eve. The people finally rising up, the cut-up flag, the crowds chanting freedom, freedom, the fall of the dictator, the intoxication of being freed from communism, heading at last towards a modern transparency, death to old-fashioned, freedom-denying principles! Drunk on their viewing figures, the Western media aren't bothered about decimal points and multiply the number of dead in Timișoara: after all, what better end to History than these corpses of Marxism–Leninism, these exemplary martyrs of a head of state whom France unfortunately decorated a few years earlier with the Grand Cross of the Legion of Honour...

Then, annoyed at not having paid close enough attention to this final communist performance, the Western judges start to condemn: that mock trial, the brutality of their killing, really, the Romanians have led off on the wrong foot in our democratic ball. The story is spoilt by their lies, those clumsily rigged photos, fake mass burials!

Verdict: 'The Romanian pseudo-revolution is just a tale. A piece of theatre put on by the Russian secret services hand-in-hand with the Americans. The Romanians themselves had little to do with it! Gorbachev had come to Bucharest two years earlier to insist on a liberalization of the regime; Ceaușescu of course dug his heels in. With the fall of the Berlin Wall and that of the surrounding communist regimes, it was unthinkable that the Old Man should remain in place. The question was not to know if he was going to fall, but how.'

And while I am taking notes on these 'incontrovertible' proofs, Nadia is the one who comes into my mind, her anger and occasionally her sorrow whenever she got the impression that I wasn't listening to what she was telling me, what she called my 'Western arrogance', my way of depicting the Eastern Bloc as a grey caricature. My embarrassed bewilderment in Bucharest as I was faced with the contrasting memories of people when I came to note down their nightmares. Nadia's weary sighs at my unwillingness to accept that the laboratory of little girls, those so-widely-condemned training methods of communist gymnasts, were perfectly copied in the West as soon as it laid its hands on their trade secrets.

The Western media manage the narrative of the Romanian revolution, a story very similar to Nadia's: numbers, judges, and all performed live. The revolution in that winter of 1989 was a fascinating globalized show, the breathless spectacle of a fall displacing that of the implacable little girls who never fell.

But what of her? What did she think of the end of that collective obedience that she witnessed in a banal way, in front of a television, in one of those American motel rooms she had to quit every morning, pursued by the press? We never discussed the strike movements in 1977 and 1987 at Braşov, those student opponents of the regime who took the delegates the Comrade sent them hostage, or those huge portraits of the Old Man found reduced to ashes in the gutters, without any or nearly any of this coming out in the rest of the country; those convulsions, small gestures constantly masked by Nadia's triumphs. How was it her fault if she was a supercharged child, a biomechanical impossibility? What did she feel the first time she saw the gaping hole between the blue, the yellow and the red, that golden badge with the red star that converted her white leotard into a target, 'Here I am, come near if you dare'. What did she think of those December days when Romania finally got its hands on its share of freedom?

I used to dream of freedom, then I arrive in the United States and say to myself: so this is freedom? I'm in a free country but I'm not free? Where then can I be free?

– Nadia C., 1989

At 12.01 on 18 July 2006, the video of your perfect performance at Montreal was broadcast by the Deep Space Communication Program, a team of engineers wanting to communicate with possible inhabitants in outer space. They claimed that these images representing 'absolute beauty' would travel through trillions of kilometres outside the solar system, for many light years.

Thirty years earlier, on 18 July 1976 in the press room at Montreal, you told the adults asking you for a thank-you and a smile that you could do all that, but only once your 'mission' was completed. Mission accomplished. No thanks or saying sorry, the little girls fling themselves into the void at the speed of a bullet of a nine-mil, their skin bare, you came to teach us what space is, you are epidemic, oh, the grand adventure.

Madame,

In the course of our conversations, you asked me for a list of my memories. If it's not too late, I should like to add this: in 1988, a handful of students circulated resistance leaflets that they signed with these words: don't look for me, because I am nowhere.

Nadia C.

Sources and references

Apart from the numerous articles, reports and documentaries devoted to the Comăneci years, any reader wishing to have more complete documentation could usefully consult:

Roxana Bobulescu, *Les Années Ceaucescu: récit d'une adolescence en Roumanie*, L'Harmattan, Paris, 2009.

Joan Chirilă, *Nadia, Gazeta Sporturilor*, Bucharest, 2009.

Nadia Comăneci, *Letters to a Young Gymnast*, Basic Books, Perseus Books Group, New York, 2011.

Béla Károlyi and Nancy Ann Richardson, *Feel No Fear: The Power, Passion and Politics of a Life in Gymnastics*, Hyperion, New York, 1996.

Adrian Neculau, *La vie quotidienne en Roumanie sous le communisme*, L'Harmattan, Paris, 2008.

John Ryan, *Little Girls in Pretty Boxes*, Grand Central Publishing, Hachette Book Group, New York, 1996.

Mihaela Wood, *Superpower: Romanian Women's Gymnastics during the Cold War*, University of Illinois, dissertation and thesis, 2010.

The author is also indebted to articles by Sorj Chalandon, Frank Deford, Jean Hatzfeld, Jean-Paul Mari, Richard Montaignac, Marc Semo.

The chapter 'Numbers' (pp. 65–66) is partially based on the documentary by Cornel Mihalache: *De Crăciun ne-am luat ratia de libertate.*

The events described in the following chapters are partially based on Nadia Comăneci's descriptions in *Letters to a Young Gymnast*, Basic Books, Perseus Books Group, New York, 2011.

'How old is she?' (p. 33)

'A contract to disobey' (p. 37)

'Béla's manipulations or plans' (p. 71)

'Monster' (p. 122)

'Please welcome the incredible Nadia' (p. 138)

'Testimony of Rodica D.' (Nadia C.'s response) (p. 143)

'Filleting the impossible' (p. 163)

'The spark' (notes on Nadia's flight) (p. 225)

The following sentences, placed in quotation marks and attributed to Nadia C. in the novel, are in part taken from Nadia Comăneci's book *Letters to a Young Gymnast* (*LYG*):

pp. 123–4: 'I'm not going to turn my back… trampling it beneath my feet' (*LYG*, p. 69)

pp. 140–1: 'I told Nadia… you can do something extraordinary' (*LYG*, p. 88)

p. 146: 'Béla pushed me a long way… I never revealed them' (*LYG*, p. 91)

pp. 219–20: 'A great floor exercise… to the judges and audience' (*LYG*, p. 115)

Acknowledgements

Thanks to Corina Oprea, who introduced me to Iulia Popovici. It was at her home in Bucharest that most of this book was written. Thank you, Iulia.

Thanks to: Alina Popescu, Andrei Nourescu, Bertille Détrie, Cristina David, Florence Illouz, Lidia Bucur, Luca Niculescu, Luminita Raileanu-Milea and her family, Marc Semo, Mihai Laurentiu Fuiorea, Miruna Mitranescu, Olivia Spătaru, Radu Paraschivescu, Sidonie Mezaize, Kyralina bookshop, the participants in the Bucharest writing workshop in April 2013.

New York, November 2012: thanks to Lise Esdaile and Ron Ottaviano.
Montreal, November 2012: thanks to Perrine Leblanc and Claude Lapointe.
To Olivier L., thanks. Because.
Thanks to Henri Lafon, Jeanne Lafon for having brought me up in Romania.
Luis P., the first reader, obviously.
To Jeanne Lafon, once again.
Isabelle Lafon, always.
To the golden team: Nadia Comăneci, Mariana Constantin, Georgeta Gabor, Anca Grigoras, Luminiţa Milea, Gabriela Trusca, Teodora Ungureanu, known as Dorina.
To the little girls of summer 1976.